Without warning, Logan moved close and grasped her chin. Lightning flickered behind him. His dark eyes seared into hers.

And then he kissed her—a deep, rough kiss that wiped out every thought.

Just as abruptly, he stepped back, grabbed the gelding's reins and turned into the turbulent night.

The wind whipped against her. Dara shivered, tightened her grip on the rope, determined to forget the kiss, forget the need sizzling in her veins, and concentrate on what mattered most—surviving the night.

They had a sniper close behind them, lightning threatening to strike, a treacherous mountain to cross.

She dragged in an unsteady breath and prepared herself to face the danger ahead.

But as she stepped into the seething night, the feel of Logan's kiss still lashing her nerves, she feared that the real danger might be the temptation brewing inside herself.

Dear Reader,

There's something about a long-lost city that really ignites my imagination. Add in towering, mist-clad mountains and ancient trails, and I'm hooked! So what better place to set this second book of THE CRUSADERS miniseries than Peru, a fascinating, profoundly spiritual land filled with pyramids, mummies, mysterious energy lines and sacred ruins.

Better yet, hiding out in the forbidding mountains I found my favorite type of hero—cynical, solitary Logan Burke. An honorable man with a wounded soul, Logan is convinced he isn't a hero. Fortunately, he's about to meet a determined princess who will prove him wrong.

I hope you enjoy their dangerous and exciting journey!

Gail Barrett

GAIL
BARRETT

To Protect a Princess

Romantic
SUSPENSE

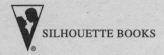 SILHOUETTE BOOKS

ISBN-13: 978-0-373-27608-0
ISBN-10:   0-373-27608-7

TO PROTECT A PRINCESS

Visit Silhouette Books at www.eHarlequin.com

Printed in U.S.A.

GAIL BARRETT

always dreamed of becoming a writer. After living
everywhere from Spain to the Bahamas, raising two
children and teaching high school Spanish for years,
she finally fulfilled that lifelong goal. Her writing has
won numerous awards, including Romance Writers of
America's prestigious Golden Heart. Gail currently
lives in western Maryland with her two sons, a quirky
Chinook dog and her own Montana rancher-turned-
retired Coast Guard officer hero. Write to her at P.O. Box
65, Funkstown, Maryland 21734-0065, or visit her Web
site, www.gailbarrett.com.

To my sister, Mary Jo Archer, for her wonderful support.

ACKNOWLEDGMENT

I'd like to give a huge thanks to author
Adrianne Lee for her brainstorming help;
farrier Kevin King for information about mules;
Darlene Leivonen for answering my endless questions
about horses; and especially Judith Sandbrook,
for her super critique help. Thank you all!

Chapter 1

Yanahirca, Peru

Trouble was coming.

The warning shivered down Logan Burke's neck like the graze of a cobweb, that whisper of *danger, danger,* he'd learned not to ignore. He knocked back his shot of whiskey, hissed as it scorched a raw, hot path through his gut, then slid his left hand to the Imbel .45 tucked into the waistband of his jeans.

The men lurking in the shadows of the cantina shifted, and the muscles along Logan's broad shoulders tensed. He eased himself into shooting position, flicked his gaze to the open door.

The newcomer stood in the doorway, backlit by sunlight, but there was no mistaking her long, slender legs and female curves.

He sucked a long, slow breath through his teeth. Trouble was right. A woman in this hellhole meant gunfights, bloodshed.

But damned if the blood would be his.

She strolled into the cantina, and the outlaws tracked her, watching her with feral eyes. These men were renegades, ex-guerrillas and terrorists hiding beyond civilization in a remote Andean village laid waste by poverty and war. Men with nothing to lose. Men waiting to die.

Men he just might have to kill.

The woman seemed oblivious to the danger. She sauntered straight toward him across the packed dirt floor, her fine-boned chin raised, the hips in those snug jeans swinging to the kind of sweet, sensual beat that compelled a man to watch. She drew closer, and he made out high, exotic cheekbones, dark, tilted eyes. And round, ripe breasts that shifted beneath her T-shirt, daring a man to touch, to taste, to take.

The men stirred. Mutters broke the tight silence. The air reeked of testosterone.

"Logan Burke?" Her voice was throaty, low-pitched. And any hope he had of avoiding trouble died.

"I'm Dara Adams." She pulled a small pack off her shoulder, held out a slender hand. The motion swept her thick, black braid past her hips.

He ignored the hand, slid his gaze across the dim room to assess the danger. Three men. Five empty bottles. Enough fire-power to run a war.

But armed or not, he knew these men wouldn't challenge him outright. They were cowards by nature, hyenas who skulked in the shadows, finding strength in packs. They'd watch, wait until they could shoot him in the back.

This woman would give them the courage to try.

She pulled her hand back. Her dark eyes flashed, and a flush climbed up her cheeks. "I need to talk to you. I heard you could help me."

"You heard wrong."

She blinked. Her sultry lips parted. "But…you don't even know what I want."

"Doesn't matter." He worked alone, lived alone, never got involved. That was the rule he lived by. The rule he'd die by.

The one rule he could never forget. His wife's death had guaranteed that.

"Of course it matters." She frowned, glanced back at the outlaws. "Can we go somewhere to talk? Alone? I have a proposition for you." She lowered her voice. "I promise it's worth your while."

The edge of his mouth ticked up. And for a second he indulged himself, letting his gaze slide over those erotic lips and creamy throat, those perfect, tempting breasts.

Hunger kicked low in his gut.

"A business proposition," she added, sounding breathless, and he tugged his gaze back up.

"Sorry. I'm not interested."

"But I've spent three weeks trying to find you." Her voice rose. "I've hiked all over Peru."

"Then you wasted your time."

"But—"

"Listen, darlin'. Let's make this clear. Real clear." He leaned close, locked his gaze on those harem eyes, tried not to inhale her female scent. "Whatever you want, the answer is no. No way in hell."

He slapped a coin on the bar, touched the brim of his leather hat, then strode across the silent room. He angled his shoulders and ducked through the open doorway, hoping she had the sense to do the same.

Because damned if he'd go back and save her.

He paused, squinted in the blazing sunshine, then headed down the dirt road to where he'd tied his horse. It didn't matter what she wanted. He knew better than to get involved with a woman like her, even for business. He'd have every renegade in Peru on his tail.

Determined to forget the woman in the bar, he strode past the crumbling huts, their thatched roofs and mud walls destroyed by warring *senderistas* and drug lords. His horse nickered, bobbed his head as he approached.

"Hey, Rupper." He rubbed the gelding's forehead and ears, grinned when the horse bumped him back. Rupe was a fifteen-hand Peruvian Paso, spirited and smart, five centuries of *brio* breeding evident in every step. And Logan hated to leave him behind on this trip. But he had a job to do—silver to haul—and he needed his sure-footed llamas for that.

He flipped a coin to the Quechua kid who'd begged to watch the horse. The boy's white teeth flashed in a smile. "*Yuspagarachu.*" Thank you. He darted off barefoot down the rutted lane.

Logan tightened the horse's cinch and checked his packs, made sure the dynamite and his AK-47 were undisturbed. He doubted anyone would have touched them. His reputation was deadly enough to keep most thieves away. But a man didn't stay alive in these mountains by letting his guard down.

His thoughts swerved back to the woman in the bar. He frowned, glanced up the empty road, and an uneasy feeling gnawed at his gut. What was she doing in the cantina for so long? He'd expected her to be out by now, heading safely down that road toward some town.

He shoved the worry aside. She wasn't his problem. He wouldn't let her be. He couldn't fail another woman like he had his wife.

And he couldn't afford to waste more time here. He glanced at the mountains looming above him, scanned the ancient Inca terraces that ringed the distant peaks. The sunshine was deceptive. The seasonal rains would hit any time now, turning the trails to mud. He'd have to hustle to get that last load of silver over the mountains before the passes closed.

Scowling, he swung himself into the saddle, nudged the gelding's flanks, and set off. The horse pranced sideways, tossed his head, oddly nervous in the quiet air, as if menace lurked in the abandoned huts.

And Logan felt just as restless. He scanned the deserted hovels, the faded graffiti on the crumbling rock walls. It was too quiet. Even the pigs and stray dogs were lying low. And that damned sense of *danger, danger* kept bludgeoning his nerves.

Then suddenly, a gunshot shattered the silence. Birds scattered and took to the sky. He jerked the rifle from his pack, wheeled his horse back toward the cantina and swore.

He'd been right. That woman was going to cause trouble.

Thank goodness she'd brought a gun.

Dara Adams stood with her back to the cantina door, her heart careening against her rib cage, the blast from her pistol still thundering in her ears. She steadied the gun in her trembling hand, took another step toward the open door.

"Stay back. *Aléjense*," she warned the three thugs who'd tried to stop her. Her shot had missed them, just taken out some bottles behind the bar. But at least it had forced them back.

But not for long.

She lifted her chin to stare them down, but their mean eyes, fueled by *pisco* and whiskey, glittered back. There were three of them, one of her. And slung over their ponchos were the deadliest weapons she'd ever seen.

They crept closer, fanning out this time, and her heart wobbled into her throat. "I said get back," she said again, sharper now, determined not to let them see her fear.

God, she didn't need this. Her forehead pounded from the too-thin air. She was spooked about the man she'd spotted following her for the past three weeks. And she was exhausted after trekking through endless villages, searching for the elusive Logan Burke.

And now that she'd finally found him, she couldn't let him get away.

She moved closer to the door, getting ready to run. But one of the outlaws lunged. She leaped back, her pulse rocketing, and raised her pistol to fire. But he caught her wrist, twisted hard, and a sharp bolt of pain shot up her arm. She gasped and dropped the gun.

He jerked her close, and she shoved back, fighting to loosen his hold. But he was strong. He pulled her tighter against him and groped her breast.

Outraged, her fear for her safety growing, she struggled to knee him, gagging on the stench of unwashed flesh. But he twisted her arm higher, trapping her against him. The men behind them laughed.

And that made her even madder. She despised bullies like this, cowards who preyed on the weak. As the Roma princess—royal representative of the Gypsies—she'd witnessed the hatred and discrimination her people endured. And she refused to let this bully win.

Furious, she struck out with her free hand, clawed at his face, slammed her hiking boot into his shin. He grunted, loosened his hold, and she managed to stumble back.

She caught her balance, her breath coming fast, but she couldn't reach her gun. The man circled her, fury contorting his face.

"*Agárrala, pendejo,*" one of the other men taunted, then laughed. And she realized with a sudden chill the danger she was in. She'd humiliated him, enraged him. And now he wanted revenge.

He leaped forward, lunged for her arm. She jumped to the side and whipped back.

"Problem, boys?" a lazy, graveled voice drawled from the doorway. The thug hesitated, looked up, and Dara's breath rushed from her lungs.

He'd come back.

She dragged in air, shook her aching wrist, took advantage of the distraction to dart over and pick up her gun. Then she turned and faced the man who'd saved her.

He filled the doorway with his muscled frame, looking every inch the desperado. His eyes were dark and grim beneath his battered hat, his mouth a lethal slash. He radiated danger, ruthlessness, from the black beard stubble darkening his rigid jaw to the assault rifle trained on the thugs. His powerful maleness made her nerves race.

Seconds passed. Tension vibrated in the stifling air.

Then suddenly, Logan's gun barked. The blast sprayed up dirt, roared in her ears, and she flinched back in shock. She gaped from Logan to the men at the bar, and the man who'd attacked her inched up his hands.

She hadn't even seen him move. But Logan had—and he'd made his point. All three men shuffled back.

"Go wait by my horse," Logan told her. His eyes never veered from the men.

She opened her mouth to argue. "Now," he added, his deep voice hard.

She stiffened. She didn't take orders, didn't let others fight her battles for her.

But then she caught the flat, mean stare of the man who'd touched her, and her dread rose. She'd made an enemy here, a dangerous one. Maybe she'd be smart to leave.

She hurried out the door into the dusty road, spotted a huge black gelding standing by some mules. His sleek coat gleamed in the sunshine. Muscles rippled in his powerful neck. He wore a worked silver browband across his strong forehead, two oiled leather packs draped over his flanks. Logan's horse. He looked as dangerous as his owner did.

Logan strode from the cantina a second later. He glanced at her, his dark eyes shadowed beneath the brim of his hat, then vaulted into the saddle and reached out his hand. "Come on."

She blinked, hesitated. "We're going to ride double?" She was a Gypsy—Roma—and proper Roma women didn't get that close to men. But then, nothing about this trip was proper.

"Unless you want to stay here."

She flicked her gaze back to the cantina, then shivered hard. "No, thanks."

She stuck her pistol in her backpack and grabbed his hand. His palm was warm, calloused, his strength impressive as he tugged her up. She swung her leg awkwardly over the horse, settling behind the saddle on the horse's rump.

"Hold on," he warned. He wheeled the horse around, and she clutched his shirt. The horse took off at a lope.

She gasped at the burst of speed, wrapped her arms around Logan's waist to keep from falling off. She buried her face in his shirt, inhaled the comforting scent of wool and man, felt his solid muscles bunch under her hands. The gelding streaked down the road, flying over rocks and ruts in easy strides, making the huts pass by in a blur.

They fled the tiny village, scaled a rocky hillside, then raced down a dusty trail. The horse's hooves drummed on the sun-baked earth. The warm wind lashed at her eyes. Minutes later, they reached a sparse stand of pine trees and slowed.

"Are you all right?" Logan asked.

"Sure." But she realized she was plastered against him, probably squeezing the air from his lungs. She pried her hands from his waist and leaned back.

But even with the added space between them, it still seemed strangely intimate to be sitting so close to him, with only the edge of the saddle separating their thighs. *Unsettling.*

But then, everything about Logan Burke unnerved her. He wasn't at all what she'd expected. When her archeologist colleague had urged her to contact him—the only man rumored to know the ancient trails—she'd envisioned a grizzled old tracker, not this virile man in his prime.

She ran her gaze over the straight black hair edging his collar beneath his hat, the strong, sinewed lines of his neck. He cradled the assault rifle in one big hand, held the reins in the other with practiced ease. He'd rolled his sleeves to his elbows, exposing tanned forearms roped with tendons. Faded jeans gloved his muscled thighs.

Flutters rose in her belly, pranced through her nerves. She couldn't deny that the man appealed to her in a very basic way.

But she'd come here to get to Quillacocha, not ogle Logan Burke. She squinted in the brilliant sunshine, gazed at the distant peaks edged with snow. The ancient city was up there in the wilderness somewhere. And only this man knew where it was.

Now she had to convince him to take her there.

They rounded the cluster of pines. Logan leaned back and hauled on the reins. The horse danced sideways and stopped.

He glanced at her over his wide shoulder. "How did you get to the village?"

"I hitched a ride partway, then hiked the rest." Her stomach growled in protest. She'd hoped to find food in the village, but the place was little more than a shelled-out ghost town. And she hadn't had a chance to eat in the bar.

He muttered something she didn't catch. "Slide off," he said. He grabbed her arm, and she dropped to the ground, then stepped away from the horse in case he kicked.

Logan leaped easily down beside her, and she realized again

how big he was. At five-six, she wasn't tiny, but she barely reached his chin. He looped the horse's reins over a branch, then strode through the trees to a rocky outcrop, still carrying his gun. She followed more slowly, rubbing her bottom and stretching her arms.

The village squatted against the mountain beneath them, its drab mud hovels devoid of life, the rutted streets deserted except for the mules tied up by the bar. Dara scanned the surrounding hillside, studied the dirt road leading into the town, then slowly hitched out her breath. Maybe she'd imagined that man following her. Maybe she'd grown paranoid after that attack in her apartment. After all, no one, except her colleague, knew where she was.

But they'd found her before, she reminded herself. Even being in protective custody after her parents' murders hadn't kept her safe. And now that she knew where that sacred dagger was...

She rubbed her pounding forehead, dropped her hand to the pack that contained the diagrams she had to protect. She'd have to watch, stay alert in case someone really had followed her into these hills.

Logan's gaze swiveled back to hers. "So, what the hell is this about?"

She chose her words carefully. It was too dangerous to tell him everything, at least for now. She only hoped he didn't hear much news out here.

"I'm an archeologist," she said, since that was true. "And I'm studying Quillacocha, the lost Inca city." That was true, too.

She shifted the pack she'd slung over her shoulder, met his relentless gaze. "I've heard that you're the only one who knows where it is. I'd like to hire you to take me there—so I can study it, take photos of the ancient tombs."

He stared at her, his dark eyes etched with disbelief. "You came all the way up here alone to see some tombs?"

Her face warmed. He made her sound foolish, reckless. As if she were really the daredevil her people believed her to be.

But she couldn't tell him the truth—about the fabled dagger, the murders, the secret society that was killing the Roma world-wide. He probably wouldn't believe her if she did.

And if he did believe her, he would never take the risk to help her. Especially if he knew who she was.

"It's important work," she argued. "Quillacocha is the link we need to understand Incan sacrificial rites. And I only need to find out where the city is, take a few photos. It won't take much of your time. I'll come back later with a team to explore it more."

His gaze pinned hers. "And it's worth risking your life to see these tombs?"

No, but finding the dagger was.

"I didn't have time to get the permits or assemble a team," she continued. There had already been too many Gypsies killed. "My colleague is working on that part. I'm going to meet up with him after I locate the tombs."

He shot her a look of incredulity, disgust, then scowled down at the village again. And she knew she hadn't convinced him. But she would. She had to. More people would die if she failed.

She took in his tall, muscular build, the barely leashed power in his dominant stance. He was a tough man, a dangerous one. A man honed for battle and ready to fight.

Exactly the man she needed up here.

And the most appealing man she'd ever seen.

A restless feeling hummed through her nerves. And she had a sudden urge to feel those hard biceps under her palms, stroke her hands up those muscled arms.

What would it be like to kiss him?

The thought sliced out of nowhere, shocking her, and she

caught her breath. Despite her sheltered upbringing as the Roma princess, she'd kissed a few men before—mostly *gadžos,* non-Roma she'd met at school. But none of them had looked like Logan Burke.

She studied the dark, hollowed planes of his face, the black beard shadow coating his jaw, the muscles of his throat. He looked disreputable, masculine. *Exciting.*

His gaze swerved to hers again, and he went still. And a sudden awareness vibrated between them, touching off the same edgy, dizzy feeling that had pulsed through her in the bar.

His gaze dropped, lingering over her lips, her breasts. Her lungs seized up. She stood cemented in place, unable to breathe. Her heart nearly beat from her chest.

And his eyes turned darker, hotter, more dangerous. As if he knew what she was thinking. As if he wanted to kiss her, too.

And then he drilled his gaze into hers. "Like I told you before, darlin'. No way in hell." He turned on his heel, strode back to his horse.

She pulled in a tremulous breath. "I'll pay you."

"I don't need your money." He strapped his rifle to his horse, adjusted a pack.

"Then why won't you help me?"

He checked the horse's cinch. "I've got commitments. I need to make another freight run over the mountains before the rains hit. And it's too dangerous."

"I'm not scared."

"You should be." His eyes snagged hers again, and shivers ran over her skin. "There aren't many women up here. You'd be a target for every renegade in Peru."

"I've made it this far. And I've got a gun."

He scoffed. "You've got no idea what you're up against."

"Sure I do." She'd faced a few tough moments on her trip

so far, but she'd survived. And she wasn't weak or afraid. "I can handle myself."

He stalked back toward her. And before she could guess his intention, he stepped close and grasped her chin. He leaned over her, so close his thighs brushed hers. Her breath backed up in her lungs.

"You think you can stop a man who wants you?" His voice was graveled now, raw, and his dark eyes burned into hers. "Hell, you think you could fight me off?"

She trembled, lost in those hot, hot eyes, the feel of his callused thumb on her throat. "You wouldn't hurt me," she whispered. "I trust you."

"Then you're a fool. Because I stopped playing the hero a long time ago." His eyes stayed on hers for a beat, long enough for her to see his anger, his desire, and then he dropped his hand and stepped back.

She swayed, shaken by the stark intensity in his hungry eyes, her nearly overpowering urge to pull him close.

"I'll take you to the next village over," he said, his voice stripped flat now. "I need to pick up my string of llamas and board my horse. Someone there can take you to a safer town."

He strode back to his horse, launched himself into the saddle, then rode up to where she still stood. He hauled her up, and she settled behind him, wrapped her arms around his back.

But if he thought she'd given up trying to convince him, he was wrong. Because her people needed that dagger. And no matter what happened, she couldn't let them down.

"Damn."

His soft curse brought her attention back to the village. "What is it?" She scanned the streets, saw the three men mounting their mules. Her pulse sped up, and she gnawed her lip. "They won't follow us, will they?"

"You can bet on it."

She swallowed, and a nervous flutter invaded her chest. She didn't need more danger dogging her trail—that mysterious man she'd glimpsed was enough. "So what are we going to do?"

"Ride like hell, darlin'."

He wheeled the horse around, prodded him into a run. But as they thundered up the road and into the mountains, she remembered the hunger in Logan's eyes, that thrilling heat.

And she wondered who was the greater threat—the outlaws or Logan Burke.

Chapter 2

If the road to Hell was paved with good intentions, Logan figured he'd just laid a long stretch of asphalt toward his final reward. He'd intended to intimidate Dara back there, make her understand that traveling in these mountains could get her killed. But he hadn't banked on that need crashing through him when he touched her—that raw, savage need that obliterated his good sense like a flash flood ravaging a rocky gorge.

And even the punishing pace he'd set through the mountains hadn't eased it. He'd driven the gelding hard—racing through empty creek beds, scrambling up the rocky terrain—but he still hadn't shaken the desire that swamped him, that hunger that pounded his blood.

He angled his horse up another steep slope. Dara leaned closer against him, and he stifled a groan. He was far too conscious of her slender arms encircling his waist, the soft breasts caressing his back.

Touching her had been a mistake all right, stirring up cravings he could never indulge in—especially with a woman like her. But he'd just have to ignore them. Once they got to that village, he could leave Dara—and temptation—behind.

It wouldn't be soon enough.

They reached an outcropping of rock above the trail, and Logan slowed. He reined the gelding to a much-needed stop, studied the thin gray slash switching across the mountain below. A mile back, some dust puffed up, then dispersed on the rising wind.

"Are they still following us?" Dara's throaty voice rippled through his nerves.

Not trusting himself to look at her, he kept his gaze on the dust. "Yeah, they're down there." And closing in fast. Too fast. *Damn.* He'd banked on their giving up. Renegades were a lazy bunch, more likely to drink themselves into a stupor than come haring after him. And this was a long, hot ride across parched terrain in the brutal, midday sun.

But Dara was a tempting prize, worth a thirsty trek through the hills.

Worth killing him for.

He hissed out his breath, turned the horse to go, but then a wisp of dust farther back caught his eye. He paused, squinted at the distant haze, and the muscles along his shoulders tensed. Had the men split up? Or was someone else out there?

He watched, narrowed his eyes. His pulse drummed a hard, slow beat. A hawk drifted past, towing a shadow over the hill. The tall grass dipped in the wind.

But nothing else moved, and he finally eased out his breath. It was probably just the wind whipping up dust, or some wild *guanaco* passing through. At least he hoped that was it. He had enough trouble on his hands with the thugs.

He glanced at the approaching men again, bit off a curse. Under normal conditions, their pack mules couldn't match his gelding's speed. But his horse was carrying a double load over steep terrain.

He kneed his horse into motion, then steered him into the brush. "What are we doing?" Dara asked.

"The trail opens up ahead. The men are less than a mile back, close enough to pick us off." Especially with the scopes they'd tooled on their Dragunov SVDs.

"So what are we going to do?"

"Take cover, wait them out. Hope they give up and turn around."

Her grip tightened on his waist. "And if they don't?"

Then he had a hell of a problem.

Refusing to think about that possibility, he urged the horse through the rocks and grass toward a pile of boulders above the trail. The wind gusted again, a cool, moisture-laden breeze that flattened the tall clumps of straw-colored grass.

He studied the rain clouds stacking up behind the peaks. A storm would hit by nightfall, he decided, the first of the season. He was going to have a hard, muddy trek through the mountains in the freezing rain—assuming he made it to the pass in time.

His gut tightened. He'd better make it. A lot of miners needed the income from that run. The starvation rate in these hills was already too damned high.

They reached a small grove of eucalyptus trees behind the boulders, and he reined in the horse. "This is good." He helped Dara dismount, then swung to the ground beside her. He pulled out his rifle, ratcheted a bullet into the chamber, nodded toward the rocks overlooking the trail. "We'll wait over there."

"Shouldn't we stay in the trees?"

"I want to know if they spot us. We'll leave Rupper here, though, so he doesn't tip off the mules."

"Rupper?" Her gaze met his. "Is that your horse's name?"

"Yeah. Rupe. Rupper." He took out an extra magazine, slid

it into his pocket, checked the position of the 9mm Imbel tucked into his jeans.

"But…that's a Romani word. Silver. Are you Roma?"

"Half," he admitted, and his gaze met hers. So she was a Gypsy. It made sense—that long, black hair, the exotic eyes. But then what was she doing out here? He hadn't been raised in the culture, but even he knew single women didn't travel alone—especially beautiful women like her.

At least he assumed she was single. He turned away, headed to the pile of boulders above the trail. She hadn't mentioned a husband, didn't wear a ring. She could be a widow. The Roma married young—too damned young. And this woman had to be in her late twenties, at least.

He reached the boulders, glanced back, watched as she sauntered toward him. And she was a marvel to watch. Her full breasts swayed, her hips swiveled like an invitation to erotic bliss. Loose strands of hair tumbled around her face, making him ache to free that silky mass, feel it sweep his chest, his thighs.

Her skin had been soft, smooth when he touched her jaw, and the memory of it flashed through his nerves. He tightened his grip on the gun, fighting the urge to reach for her again, to test the weight of her breasts.

He sucked in his breath, hissed it out. She was something, all right. No wonder those renegades hadn't given up yet.

But single or not, she was none of his business. She'd asked for his help, and he'd refused. End of story. Now he just had to drop her off at that village and be on his way.

And keep his hands off her until he did.

He leaned over the boulders, spotted the dust rising on the trail. "They're still a few minutes back." He lowered himself to the ground, leaned against the rocks to wait. Dara sat down beside him.

She drew her gun from her bag, settled back against the rock, mimicking him. He eyed the small pistol in her hands. "You know how to shoot that thing?"

"I do all right."

"*All right* doesn't cut it out here."

She lifted her chin, and her sultry eyes met his. "Don't worry. I can defend myself."

Right. "Like you did in the bar?"

A flush climbed up her cheeks. "I was caught off guard. It won't happen again."

"Damn right it won't." Because she'd be back to civilization before nightfall. He'd make sure of that.

"I'm serious about the dangers," he told her, in case she had plans to continue alone. "These mountains are filled with outlaws—drug runners bringing down coca leaves, ex-revolutionaries, Shining Path and Túpac guerrillas with nowhere else to hide. And the law doesn't mean squat out here. Strength rules, bribes pay for silence, no matter what you've done. Even murderers walk free."

Especially if they'd only killed a Gypsy.

His belly clenched. And before he could block it, the frustration and rage surged back—rage at the corruption, the injustice, at a world where money ruled, where no one cared, where the innocent always died. But he dragged in air, forced the painful past from his mind. This wasn't the time to dwell on his dead wife.

"Then there are wild animals, pumas," he continued. "No doctors, no clinics, not even a Quechua shaman for miles. Even a minor injury or infection can do you in. And those tombs you want to see are at sixteen thousand feet. You'd be lucky to survive the thin air."

Her eyes met his. "You survive out here."

"I've spent most of my life in these hills. You haven't." He held her gaze, making sure she understood. "I'm not kidding, Dara. A woman like you doesn't belong here."

"How do you know?" Her chin lifted in challenge. "You don't know anything about me."

He knew enough. And he wouldn't hang around to find out more.

His horse lifted his head then, and he rose. "Stay down," he warned. "Don't make a sound." He leaned against the rocks, trained the AK-47 on the trail.

But Dara stood and squeezed in beside him, her shoulder touching his arm. He shot her a scowl. Hadn't she heard him? She should be plastered against the rocks, praying those renegades didn't spot her. But she aimed her gun, looking cool as hell.

He swore, hoped she had the sense to hold her fire, then jerked his attention back to the trail. The three outlaws rode into view, just a few yards below where they stood.

The men had their Dragunovs strapped over their ponchos, more weapons within easy reach. Ready to fight. His hope that they would give up and turn back started to fade.

Then the wind shifted. The lead mule pricked up his ears, lifted his head, and Logan tensed. The wind was blowing their scent toward the mules. But the mule settled down, the men rode past in a haze of dust, and he eased out his breath.

He touched Dara's arm, signaled for her to keep still. She nodded that she understood. He kept his rifle aimed on the men.

The outlaws crested the hill, came to a stop. They looked around, scanned the open valley ahead.

Come on, he silently urged them. *You've lost our trail. Turn back.*

He waited, barely breathing, his blood pumping a loud, rough beat through his skull. Because if those outlaws didn't give up, if they rode on to that next village...

He could never leave Dara there, not with those men around. He'd be condemning another woman to die. Not that they'd kill her outright—although it would be kinder if they did. By the time they finished with her, she wouldn't want to survive.

And she wouldn't be the only one at risk. Those men would slaughter anyone in the village who tried to stop them.

The outlaws scoured the trail, searched for tracks. A deep sense of dread tightened his throat, like a steel trap locking him in. He couldn't go forward, couldn't take her back.

So what could he do? Take her with him into the hills? Take responsibility for another woman's life?

No way.

No damned way.

He swore under his breath, turned the dilemma over in his head, tried to come up with another plan. But there was no way out. Unless those outlaws turned around, he'd be stuck.

The men turned back, headed toward him, and his hopes picked up. But they were riding slowly, too slowly, still hunting for tracks. His gut tensed. Sweat trickled down his unshaven jaw.

The men reached the trail directly below them, and the rising wind gusted again. The lead mule stopped and bobbed his head.

The mule's rider looked up, squinted at the rocks. "*¡Allá! Up there!*" he yelled and raised his gun.

Logan dove, yanking Dara down with him. Shots riddled the boulder above their heads. "Get into the trees," he ordered, his pulse hammering fast now. He waited a beat, rose, fired off a volley of rounds to pin them down. "Damn it! Run!"

Out of the corner of his eye, he saw her move. He ducked, slapped another magazine in the AK-47, leaped up and shot again. While she fled, he blasted away at the outlaws, giving her time to reach the trees. Then he stopped and raced to his horse.

"Stay in the trees," he shouted to her as he grabbed the

reins. "I'll get you." He vaulted into the saddle, spun around, fired toward the boulders to keep down the thugs. Then he urged the horse toward the trees.

But Dara leaped into the open, and his heart kicked. "Get back!" he yelled as he charged toward her. She ignored him, pointed her pistol toward the rocks, and opened fire.

Fear seized his throat. The reckless fool! Did she have a death wish? Outraged, so angry his vision blurred, he spurred the horse to where she stood. She stopped shooting, grabbed his hand, and he yanked her up.

"Are you out of your mind?" he raged as she clutched his shirt. "Why didn't you stay back?"

"They were climbing the rocks. They would have killed you."

So she'd put herself in danger instead. Furious, he glanced toward the boulders, ripped off several more rounds, then swung the horse around and galloped off.

Still swearing, he kicked the horse into a flat-out run, racing through the woods toward the river gorge. He'd deal with Dara later, make damned sure she listened to him next time.

If there was a next time. Unless they got to the gorge and crossed that bridge before the renegades did, they'd both be dead.

He nudged the gelding, forcing him to keep to the breakneck speed. But a sense of finality, of relentless inevitability, seeped through the adrenaline like a noose tightening around his neck. Once he crossed that bridge, he couldn't turn back. It would take him miles out of his way, put an end to his plans to make that silver run.

And he'd be out in these mountains with a woman alone, her safety in his hands.

Again.

The one thing he'd vowed to never do.

Fury mixed with dread, burned through his gut. Then a

sharp crack sounded behind him, and he swerved. A gunshot—or maybe it was the sound of fate laughing at him, mocking his plight.

Another woman. Another trek through the wilderness. Another chance to fail.

His worst nightmare come to life.

Chapter 3

Dara clung to Logan's waist as they zigzagged down the side of a mountain, then hurtled along the cliff above a rocky gorge. Her heart pounded, her blood roaring louder than the river slamming the boulders below.

She braved a quick glance back, squinted in the tearing wind, but couldn't see the outlaws yet. Logan had raced full out down the steep slope to avoid their gunfire, but they couldn't be too far behind.

"When we reach the bridge, get off," Logan shouted over his shoulder. "You cross first. I'll be behind you with the horse."

"Can't we ride across?" she shouted back, but the wind whipped the words from her mouth. Then the bridge came into view, and the shock of it made her breath stall.

It was a dilapidated rope suspension bridge—a sagging mass of woven grass cables stretching two hundred feet over the plunging gorge. The ropes had darkened, loosened with age, unraveling at the bottom and sides, creating gaps wide enough to fall through. The entire structure drooped, forming a dangerous, gap-riddled vee that swung precariously in the wind.

And a hundred feet beneath it, the rapids raged.

Oh, God.

Disbelief gripped her. Anxiety tightened her nerves. Would that bridge hold their weight? Not that they had much choice with the outlaws closing in fast. And Logan wouldn't cross if it wasn't safe.

Would he?

He hauled up on the reins, jerked the horse to a stop at the edge of the cliff, and she leaped down. "Run," he urged her. "I'll be behind you."

"Right." She raced to the bridge, paused at the edge—and took in the sheer, dizzying drop, the water crashing furiously below, the high wind making the long bridge sway. Her head grew light. Panic strangled her throat.

This probably wasn't a good time to mention that she hated heights.

She swung her backpack over her shoulder, grabbed the thick grass cables that served as handrails on each side. The bridge was narrow, sagging so badly she could hardly squeeze herself through.

Her pulse jittered hard. She struggled to breathe, but it was like trying to pull a wad of cotton through a needle's eye. She stepped onto the bridge, felt it tremble beneath her feet.

"Go on!" Logan shouted behind her, and she glanced back. He had dismounted, stood holding the reins, and she saw the urgency etched on his face. Could the horse really make it over these ropes? Could she?

There was only one way to find out.

She jerked her gaze back to the bridge, forced her feet to move, trying desperately to ignore the water roaring under the gaps. The ropes felt slick in her sweaty palms, and she tightened her grip on the sides.

She could do this. She *had* to do this.

Maybe if she just darted across…

She took several fast steps, determined to hurry, but the bridge rippled and swayed underfoot. And then it jolted hard, dipped dangerously, nearly knocking her off her feet. She gasped, glanced back, saw Logan on the bridge with the horse.

"Hurry up," he shouted. He kept coming towards her, leading the balking horse, but the added weight made the bridge lurch.

Her legs quivering wildly now, feeling as disjointed as a marionette in amateur hands, she tried to balance on the bouncing ropes. She fixed her gaze on the opposite side, headed downhill into the sagging center of the bridge, afraid the river was sucking her in.

But she couldn't panic, couldn't succumb to the fear. They had to escape those men.

And she couldn't let Logan think she was weak. She'd spent too many years not measuring up, never meeting people's expectations, especially her father's. It had killed her to see that pained disappointment in his eyes.

And now this man thought she couldn't cope.

She would prove him wrong. She'd prove everyone wrong. Her people needed her; she was the only royal left. She had to help them survive. But to do that, she had to cross this bridge.

She reached the lowest point of the span, kept her eyes off the river churning through the gaps, and started up the opposite side. The climb was steep, and the wind gusted, making the treacherous bridge sway hard. She jerked her eyes from the rapids frothing beneath her, slid her shaking hands over the ropes. It wasn't much farther. She was almost there.

She rushed the final distance, leaped onto solid ground.

Relief sapped her strength, turning her head light. She nearly collapsed and kissed the earth.

But those outlaws were behind them. She whirled back, her pulse sprinting again, scanned the slope across the gorge. There was still no sign of the men, so for the moment, at least, they were safe.

Logan led the anxious horse off the bridge and stopped beside her. "Here, hold this." He handed her the reins.

She grabbed the leather straps, eyed the trembling horse, while Logan rummaged through one of his packs. "I'm going to blow up the bridge," he told her. He pulled out a stick of dynamite, a fuse, and then his eyes pinned hers. "Take Rupper behind that hill, and wait for me there. And hold on to him. I don't want him to spook when this thing blows."

"But what about you?" Her stomach balled in a rush of nerves. "Where will you be?"

"I'll be there as soon as I set the charge." He closed the flap on his pack, jogged back to the bridge. She opened her mouth, wanting to protest, but they did need to protect the horse. She dithered for a moment, reluctant to leave Logan, and finally led the gelding toward the rocky hill. She'd tie up the horse and come back.

But then a bullet whined past.

Her pulse jerked, slammed to a halt. She whipped around, saw their pursuers racing down the opposite hill.

And Logan was out on the bridge, exposed.

She had to protect him. She couldn't let him die!

She hurried the horse around the rocks, scanned the steep slabs of granite rising toward the towering peaks, but there were no trees, no place to tie him up. "Stay," she told him firmly, and hoped he obeyed. Logan wouldn't thank her if she lost his horse.

But the horse wouldn't matter if he died.

She jerked her pistol from her pack, raced back to the bridge.

The gorge was two hundred feet across, too far for her to shoot with any accuracy.

And those men had rifles. The distance wouldn't be a problem for them. Logan didn't stand a chance—especially while he was setting that charge.

She had to get closer, provide cover. She had to creep out onto the bridge again, take advantage of the sagging center to shoot over Logan's head.

She choked back the dread, refused to think about the precarious ropes. She kept the pistol in one hand, clutched the grass cable with the other, then forced herself onto the bridge. It bounced and swayed in the wind.

The outlaws had dismounted on the other side now. Logan was kneeling about five yards out, setting his charge beyond the massive stone pylons that anchored the bridge to the cliff.

One man raised his rifle, and her heart seized up. She whipped up her gun, fired a shot in their direction, praying it would worry them enough to drive them back.

Logan's head jerked up. "Get out of here!" he yelled. He lit the fuse, started running toward her. The ropes beneath her bounced.

More gunshots barked, and her nerves went wild. The only way to shoot back and miss Logan was to lean out over the gorge. She eyed the spaces between the ropes, the water rocketing below, and her heart made a crazy dip.

But she had to do it. She couldn't let those outlaws win. She sucked in her breath, leaned against the side rope, aimed toward the opposite cliff. She fired, fired again. She missed, but the thugs dispersed.

Then she struggled to pull herself upright, but Logan was running toward her, making the ropes jump under her feet. She slipped, shrieked, fell against the handrail. One leg slid through a gap.

Her heart spasmed. Time stalled.

But Logan grabbed her arm and yanked her up. "Go!" he shouted and pushed her forward. "Go, go, go!"

She raced off the bridge, headed for the rocks. Panic fueled her steps.

And then the dynamite blew.

The explosion boomed, jolted the ground, and she staggered, lost her balance, nearly fell. And then a bigger blast roared in her ears.

Logan shoved her against the rocks, flattened himself against her, covering her body with his. The ground vibrated, reverberated through her feet, rumbling into a fierce drum that rattled her chest.

Her face was mashed against Logan's chest. Sharp stones dug into her back. The explosion crackled, zinged like bullets firing around them, and then dirt drizzled onto their heads.

He leaned harder against her, sheltering her head with his arms, protecting her from the falling debris. And she clutched his arms, digging her fingers into his biceps, trying to curl herself into his skin.

Long moments later, the noise finally faded, and the echo in her ears began to ease. "Is it over?" she asked, her heart still racing.

"Yeah."

She dragged at the dusty air and coughed. God, that was close. He could have died out there with those outlaws firing at him—and it would have been her fault. But he was safe now, safe. She shivered hard, tried to calm her quivering heart.

But he still didn't move. And she was suddenly aware of how close he was. His muscled thighs crowded hers, his strong arms bracketed her head. He smelled safe, strong—like dusty flannel and warm male skin. His ragged breath fanned her neck.

Her pulse sped up. Her shaky breath snagged in her lungs. She could feel the heat of him through the layers of clothes, the hard muscles pressed against hers.

Hard everything. The intimacy shocked her, excited her. And then he shifted, and a sudden heat shot through her blood.

She tightened her grip on his arms. He slowly lifted his head.

His dark eyes locked on to hers. He was close, so close. And she gazed back at him, trapped by the dark, raw heat in his eyes. She traced the hollows of his face, the black scruff coating his jaw, that sexy, masculine mouth. His hat had fallen off, and his thick, black hair was wild now, dusted with dirt. The sheer maleness of him made her nerves rush.

His gaze dropped to her lips and stalled. Her breath grew erratic, her blood skipped crazily through her veins. And then his gaze caught hers, and she was lost in those dark, dark eyes.

"Damn," he muttered, and slanted his head. And then his lips claimed hers. She stiffened, electrified by the feel of his mouth on hers, the rasp of his whiskered cheek. Thrills rose from her belly, shot through her nerves.

He placed his hand on her jaw, changed the angle of his mouth, ran his tongue along her closed lips. Pleasure spiraled through her, and she gasped.

He slipped his tongue inside her mouth, aligned her closer against him. And her body exploded with sensation, fierce waves of it, like aftershocks from that dynamite blast.

Stunned, feeling as if she'd vaulted back into that explosion, she clung to his biceps, slid her hands up those massive arms. He made a low, rough sound, pulled her hips tighter against him. And pleasure burst through her at the intimate contact, shocking, drugging pleasure, making her want to get closer, then closer yet.

Her knees trembled. Her head whirled as he deepened the kiss, sweeping her mouth with his tongue. She'd never felt anything so wild, so glorious. *So free.*

She moaned, wanting more. Needing more. She was lost. She didn't care. She didn't want these feelings to end.

But he pulled back and lifted his head. His uneven breath mingled with hers. And she could only stare back at him, shocked, stunned, amazed.

He dropped his hands and stepped back, his gaze still burning on hers. And then he turned, picked up his hat, his movements slow, stiff. He banged the hat on his thigh to dislodge the dust, shoved it back onto his head.

His gaze cut to hers again, and she knew instantly that something had changed. His eyes were still hot, still narrowed, but not just with hunger now.

He was furious. The anger vibrated right out of him and charged through the air.

Her heart plunged. She knew what he was thinking. That kiss had been reckless, wildly inappropriate. She'd broken every Roma rule.

Daredevil, her people called her. Too impulsive to be a princess. Maybe they were right.

A lifetime of condemnation swept through her, and her face flamed. She hugged her arms, searched for something to say. "Is…is the bridge gone?"

His mouth flattened more, carving deep brackets in those heavily stubbled cheeks. "Hell if I know." His voice was bitter, rough. "But my sanity sure is."

He turned, stalked around the rock in the direction of the bridge, anger pounding his strides.

She hitched out her breath and watched him go. But her mind was still spinning, her body pulsing from that delirious kiss.

Oh, God. She pressed her fingers to her lips, sagged back against the rocks. That kiss had been wrong, she knew that. Wrong for a princess. Wrong for a respectable Gypsy woman. Wrong, wrong, wrong.

But heaven help her, she didn't care. She only wanted to kiss him again.

Chapter 4

He'd lost his mind. He'd gone over the edge, spiraled out of control, broken his most critical rule.

"I'm sorry about your horse," Dara said from beside him as they hiked up the trail from the bridge.

Logan grunted. The missing gelding was the least of his problems right now.

"You don't think he's lost, do you?"

"He won't go far." His words came out brusque, rougher than he'd intended, and he clamped his already rigid jaw. She didn't deserve his bad temper. It wasn't her fault he'd lost his self-control.

But damn, he was angry. Angry that he couldn't complete that freight run. Angry that he was trapped in the mountains with another vulnerable woman. Angry that he'd given in to the insane desire to kiss her.

And hungered to do it again.

He hissed, struggled to get a hold on his ragged temper as he strode up the dusty path. What was wrong with him? Bad enough that he was stuck with her for the next few days, that he was responsible for keeping her safe. He couldn't compound the problem by doing something he would regret.

His body wouldn't regret it.

He slid his gaze to her sweet, full breasts, and his blood surged. This woman had riveted him since the moment he'd seen her. And she'd felt better than he'd imagined—soft, sultry. And the way she'd reacted to that kiss, shivering, rocking against him, making him burn for more.

Disgusted at himself, he picked up his pace on the rocky slope, battled the need that pounded his veins. So they had chemistry. Staggering chemistry. The kind of chemistry that tempted a man to break every rule and blind himself to the past.

It didn't matter.

He had no business touching Dara. Not now. Not ever. She was off-limits to him. *Prohibida.*

And they had a treacherous trek ahead of them. It would take days of hard riding to get her across the mountain to another town. He couldn't afford a distraction that could get them killed.

He lifted his head, determined to get his mind on track, but a flash of light across the river made him stop. He frowned, focused on the trees crowning the opposite ridge, felt the skin shiver in the back of his neck. Was someone there? Those renegades should have given up, headed down to a village by now. Or had he only imagined that flash?

The wind rose, keening through the stark stone canyon, spiking the air with the threat of rain. He narrowed his gaze on the woods, remembered the plume of dust he'd seen on the trail.

And a deep sense of foreboding rippled through him. He wasn't a fanciful man. He'd bet his gelding there was someone else on that ridge. Which meant he had to keep his wits about him—and end this madness with Dara now.

He turned his attention to the woman beside him. The breeze whipped her silky hair loose, and she tucked the stray strands behind her ears.

"Look, Dara." Her eyes swiveled to his, and he gentled his voice. "I'm sorry about that—" that moment of mind-blasting pleasure "—for what happened back there."

A blush flared on her cheeks, turning her skin a dusty rose, and she folded her arms under her breasts. "It wasn't your fault."

"Sure it was." He could have—should have—stepped away. He rubbed the back of his neck, appalled by how badly he'd lost control. "It won't happen again."

"I understand."

She sounded hurt, not relieved, and he frowned. "Do you?"

"Sure." Her gaze skidded away. "You thought I was reckless."

He bit off a laugh. "Darlin', that was the entire problem. I wasn't thinking at all. You made me burn."

Her blush deepened, but her eyes locked on his. "I did, too," she whispered. "I thought it was…amazing."

Heat rushed to his loins. A hot surge of hunger clawed at his gut. And the desire to go to her, to stroke those soft, ripe curves, to ravage her lips, her mouth, slammed through him so hard that his hands shook.

He hauled in a breath to cool his blood, but he couldn't disguise the need in his eyes, the ache that was pounding his veins. Everything male in him reacted to the promise in her voice, that kiss.

Against his better judgment, he stepped close, too close, forcing her to look up to meet his eyes. He inhaled her scent, felt heat rising from her velvet skin, hungered to bury himself in her warmth. "You're playing with fire, darlin'." His voice scraped the quiet air.

He reached out, stroked his palm up that silky throat, traced the delicate line of her jaw. Her breath hitched, her pulse stumbled under his thumb, sending a rush of lust through his blood. And her dark, wild eyes stayed locked on his—mesmerizing, aroused.

Fire blazed inside him, a deep, carnal pull that incinerated his nerves. "But be damned careful what you offer," he warned her, and his voice turned huskier still. "Because I'll take it. Don't think I'm better than any other man."

Especially when they were out here alone.

Her gaze dropped to his mouth, flicked back up. Desire burned in those witchy eyes, along with a hint of doubt. And that stopped him. He despised losing control, liked being manipulated even less.

He dropped his hand, stepped back, putting some badly needed air between them. He knew all about guilt. He dreamed it, breathed it, shouldered the crushing weight of it day after relentless day. And he'd be damned if he'd add more regrets to the list.

No matter how tempting this woman was.

His temper rising again, he turned on his heel, tried to pull his mind away from the need. She'd been warned. Now he had more important things to worry about, like how to keep her safe.

The trail wound along the bluff above the plunging gorge, through tall, parched clumps of grass. He picked up the pace, anxious to find his horse, feeling too exposed on the open cliff.

But then another flash of light caught his eye.

He stopped, scanned the opposite cliff. He hadn't imagined that flash this time. That had been sunlight glinting off glass.

He watched, his lungs still now, his pulse drumming a slow, steady beat. The wind teased the hairs on the nape of his neck, ruffled the tufts of dried grass. There was no movement, no sign of life on the opposite ridge.

"What's wrong?" Dara asked, stopping beside him. "Are those men still there?"

"I doubt it." He didn't move his gaze from the trees. "They're probably heading to the nearest bar by now." They'd lie in wait, drink up their courage, plan to ambush them when they came off the hills.

Someone was out there, though. He knew it, as surely as he knew how to breathe. He scanned the cliffs again, the sun-baked earth sloping to the blown-up bridge. Nothing moved. But he'd learned the hard way not to ignore his instincts. And his nerves screamed that someone was on their trail.

Someone more deadly than the local thugs.

"Is it…there isn't someone else out there?"

He caught the anxiety in her voice, and his heart rolled. He shifted his gaze to her. "You have reason to think there'd be?"

"No." Her dark eyes slid from his.

Was she lying? He studied the nervous pull of her lips, the worry creasing her delicate brow. And his suspicion rose. If she'd led him into a trap…

"It doesn't matter, does it?" she asked, her voice pitched higher now. "I mean, nobody can get across since you blew up the bridge."

"There's another place," he said, still not taking his eyes off her. "Another bridge about an hour ahead."

She nibbled her lip, met his gaze, the worry clear in her eyes. "And someone could cross there?"

"Maybe. It's on an old trail. Most people don't know it exists." And the bridge hadn't been maintained in decades, not since a landslide blocked it off. It would take a desperate man to try to cross.

But he knew all about desperation, the lengths it could drive a man. And if someone was out there, he needed to know. Only a fool headed into these mountains unaware.

He wasn't a fool. And he wouldn't let any woman, no matter how appealing, turn him into one.

But he was a man without a horse, without supplies.

Without much time.

"Come on." He turned abruptly, stalked up the slope, shot a frown at the darkening sky. Storm clouds were moving into position over the mountains now, their lead-lined bottoms edging out the vibrant sky. And rain could be deadly out here, bringing on flash floods and mudslides. But they needed to find out who they were up against before they headed to higher ground.

Dara caught up with his long strides a second later. They walked in silence up the slope, their boots thudding on the hard dirt. "So how do you know about the bridge?" she asked.

He reined in the suspicion building inside, slid her a glance. If she was lying, he'd find out soon enough. "I use the old trails when I'm hauling silver or gold."

"You're a miner?"

"No. I'm not that desperate." *Not anymore.*

"What do you mean?"

He paused, whistled for the gelding, then caught up to her again. "You've never seen a mining town? They're slums," he told her when she shook her head. "Worse than slums. There's no running water, no sanitation, no laws. Just violence and disease. Mercury poisons the water, the air. Human waste runs in open pits down the roads."

His mind flashed to the squalor and suffering, the dull hopelessness in the children's eyes. The same blank look he would have had in his eyes if he'd stayed.

He thinned his lips. "The mines are worse. They're not fit for animals. The operations up here aren't modern, and there aren't safety regulations or laws—at least none they enforce. Tunnels collapse. Men die. The miners chew coca leaves all day so they'll be numb enough to dig."

"But...that's awful," she said, and stopped. And he saw the horror in her eyes, the shock. "Why would anyone live like that?"

"Desperation." A feeling he knew well. "They either dig or die. There's nothing else they can do."

Her gaze stayed on his for a beat, and something moved in her eyes, a glimmer of understanding, empathy. She looked away.

They started walking again, and for a long moment neither spoke. Their footsteps crunched on the hard dirt path. A hawk glided past, then banked on a current of air. "Is that why you have the dynamite?" she finally asked. "For the miners?"

"Yeah. I haul the finished metal down to the nearest town and bring back supplies. I was supposed to meet a miner in that village, but he didn't show."

Her gaze slid to the pistol tucked into the waistband of his jeans, and a small crease furrowed her brow. "Your job sounds dangerous."

He shrugged. "Most men leave me alone."

Instead, they'd attacked his wife.

The thought barreled out of nowhere, catching him off guard, and he scowled. He never dwelled on the past, never discussed his wife. He didn't have to. He would carry the burden of her death until he died.

"Logan." Dara touched his sleeve, and he stopped, looked into her sultry eyes. "I'm sorry. I really am. I didn't mean to cause problems for the miners or keep you from your job."

The concern in her eyes drew him in, pulling him deeper, sparking a flicker of warmth in his chest, the flame of a long-buried need. Tempting him to move closer, to surround himself with her gentleness, her sympathy, her ease.

He shook himself, jerked his gaze away.

But he had to admit she seemed to care, more than his wife ever had. María had hated the mountains, resented the time he'd spent away from her, blamed him for taking her from the city she loved.

In the end, she'd been right to despise him. He'd failed to protect her. He'd let her die. Hell, he'd even failed to find the men who'd killed her. Her murderers still walked free.

And now he had another woman's life in his hands.

The earth vibrated under his feet then, and the drumming of hooves interrupted his thoughts. Tension whipped through him, and he grabbed her arm. "Back here." Moving quickly, he jerked her behind a boulder beside the trail.

"Isn't that your horse?" she whispered as he pushed her down.

"Maybe." But he wouldn't take any chances until he was sure. He blocked her from view, tugged the pistol from his jeans, took position behind the rock. But she pulled out her own gun, and he shot her a warning glance. She'd better not do anything rash. That had been damned reckless behavior back at the bridge.

Behavior he'd better nip fast.

The gelding trotted into view, and she started to rise. "Wait." He clamped his hand on her shoulder and held her down.

The gelding scented them, came to a halt, but Logan didn't move. He kept his eyes on the trail, listened hard. The cool wind brushed his face. Sparrows chirped from a nearby bush. When a chinchilla crept into the path, he finally let Dara go.

"It's clear. Hey, Rupe." He tucked his pistol away, strode to the horse.

"Is he all right?" Dara asked from behind him.

He circled the gelding and checked his hooves, eyed the lather dried on his coat. "Nothing a brush won't fix."

"I'm glad." She reached out and stroked the gelding's nose. "He's a gorgeous horse."

"He's smart, loyal. That's more important than looks." In horses or people.

Another lesson he'd learned the hard way.

He checked the cinch, the packs, then glanced at Dara again. Her cheeks were flushed. Shadows smudged the skin around her eyes. Loose strands of hair had escaped her braid, and gleamed like black silk against her neck.

She looked weary, disheveled. His sympathy rose, but he quickly crushed it down. He couldn't afford to indulge her. He couldn't even fully trust her. They had a long, dangerous trek through the mountains before he could get her to a decent town.

Time to make that clear.

"You're in for a rough ride," he warned. "The trails are narrow and steep, the air thin enough to make your lungs burst. And the rains are coming. That's going to make it miserable, muddy, and cold."

Her full lips flattened. "Don't worry. I can make it."

"And there isn't much food. I work alone, so I don't carry extra supplies. So if you've got some Roma rule about sharing food, you're out of luck."

"I said I can make it. I'm stronger than you think." She lifted her chin, and challenge glinted in her velvet eyes. "And I've never been one to follow the rules."

Heat bolted through him, and he scowled. This wasn't the time to remember their kiss. "You'll follow my rules. We're not playing around out here. A mistake in these mountains can get you killed."

She straightened her back, opened her mouth as if to protest, but he drilled his gaze into hers. "I mean it, Dara. When I say run, you run. That was damned reckless what you did at the bridge. You either obey my orders or you're on your own."

He saw the mulish look in her eyes, but he held her gaze, making sure she understood. Survival wasn't a game. He'd seen too many people die to play around. She finally flushed and looked away.

Satisfied, he held out his hand. "Give me your bag. I'll tie it on the horse."

"I'm fine."

"Suit yourself." Not willing to waste more time, he swung himself into the saddle, then reached down and hauled her up.

She settled behind him, and he wheeled the horse around, then urged him into a lope—and tried not to think about the soft curves pressed to his back, the ecstasy of that kiss. Because he wasn't kidding about the urgency. If there really was someone out there, he needed to find out fast.

He pressed the horse into a gallop, depending on the hard ride to keep his mind on track. But despite the danger, despite the pace, his unruly mind kept veering to the swell of her breasts, to the soft, moist heat of her mouth, returning to that kiss again and again.

And he couldn't help wondering how much experience she had—or which rules she'd be willing to break.

By the time they reached the bluff above the abandoned bridge an hour later, his frustration was reaching the flash point. He slowed the horse, then reined him in by a eucalyptus tree, glad for the short reprieve. "We'll stop here for a minute."

He helped her off, winced when she staggered away from the horse. But he bit back his words of sympathy. She might be stiff now, but the ride would get harder yet.

He leaped down after her, pulled his binoculars and rifle from the pack, while she hobbled toward a bush. He didn't loosen the gelding's cinch. If someone was out there, they had to be ready to ride.

His nerves ratcheted tight now, he crept as close to the edge of the cliff as he dared, and crouched behind a rock. The canyon was deep, hedged in by bluffs stripped bare by the constant wind. A hundred feet below him, the ancient rope bridge swayed over the plunging gorge like a stringy, tattered net.

Still using the boulder to shield him, he rose, scanned the opposite ridge for signs of life, careful not to let the afternoon sun catch the binoculars' lens. The trail leading down to the bridge was steep, treacherous even before the landslide had blocked it off. Now it would be suicidal to even try.

He charted a path through the landslide debris, angled the binoculars down.

And stopped. Right there, picking his way through the rubble, was a man leading a mule.

Logan's lungs went still. He zeroed in on the man, noted the ammo pouches on his assault vest, the Dragunov sniper rifle slung over his chest. Former military. Moved like a professional.

And he'd come armed to kill.

Logan didn't believe in coincidence. That man was hunting them. But why? The dynamite in his packs wasn't worth much, except to the miners who needed supplies. And he wasn't hauling silver or gold.

Which left the woman.

His mouth thinned. The renegades wanted her for obvious reasons. There weren't many females around. And a terrorist might try to hold her for ransom, to fund some personal war. But a sniper? Why would a sniper pursue an archeologist?

Unless the woman had lied.

Her footsteps crunched behind her, and he rose. His face burning, so angry he couldn't speak, he seized her arm and yanked her back through the trees, his vision hazing with every stride.

"What's wrong?" she asked, sounding breathless. She trotted beside him to keep up. "Is someone there?"

"You might say that." He stalked to the horse and released her arm, his blood rushing hard through his skull.

She'd lied. The damned woman had lied. Just what the hell was she up to?

"So what are you going to do?" she asked, her voice anxious, high. "Blow up the bridge?"

"No." The cliff was too unstable, too exposed. And that sniper would pick him off before he could set the charge.

Which left two choices. They either outran that man or they died.

He sprang into the saddle, jerked her up behind him. "We're going to ride hard," he warned. "You can use the time to think."

"Think?" Her hands clutched his waist.

"About the truth." He twisted in the saddle, and his gaze nailed hers. "Because when we stop, you're going to tell me what you're really doing out here."

Chapter 5

Dara had never seen a more furious man. Tension vibrated off Logan's shoulders and powerful back as he stood in the rocky ravine, watering his horse at the creek. His jaw was clamped in a rigid line, his profile as unyielding as the granite slabs on the towering peaks. Anger simmered in every move.

The cool wind gusted up the narrow canyon with a rumble of thunder, and she shivered and rubbed her arms. For the past two hours they'd climbed at a reckless pace, cutting across plunging hillsides, backtracking through shallow stream beds, edging around valleys so steep she'd grown dizzy when she'd braved a glimpse down.

And Logan hadn't spoken the entire time. He'd been restless, alert, checking frequently for signs of pursuit, his AK-47 at hand.

The thunder rolled again, drumming through her aching forehead, and she glanced uneasily at the darkening sky. The land had stilled, the air hushed as the storm approached, turning as ominous as Logan's temper.

And just as ready to explode.

He left the creek and prowled back to her then, leading his hulking horse. She eyed the barely leashed power in his forceful strides, the dark eyes burning beneath the brim of his weathered hat.

And a sudden flutter skimmed through her nerves, hummed in her blood. Angry or not, everything about this man appealed to her. Just the memory of that kiss made her body pulse with heat.

He stepped close, forcing her to look past his steel-hard chest to meet his eyes. And that virile maleness swamped over her again, that electric awareness that made her forget to breathe. She pressed her hand to her belly to quiet her nerves.

"All right, let's have it." His deep voice broke the charged silence. "What are you doing out here? And I want the truth this time."

She turned to the gelding, stroked the elegant nose sloping beneath the silver brow band, buying time while she chose her words. Her colleague had warned her not to tell anyone about the dagger, not even Logan Burke. The danger of theft was far too great.

But Logan didn't care about treasure. He helped the miners, made a living hauling silver and gold. She slid him a glance, eyed the taut grooves bracketing his masculine mouth, the implacable planes of his face. And she knew that she could trust him. This man was honest, honorable. She felt it down to her bones.

"I told you I need to find Quillacocha, the lost Inca city," she said. "And that's true. I do need to find it. But not to study the tomb. I'm looking for the dagger, the Roma dagger. The one from the legend—the Gypsy's Revenge."

He didn't blink, didn't move. He continued to watch her,

alert, intent, like a dangerous predator studying his prey. Only a slight narrowing at the corners of his eyes indicated he'd heard.

"You probably know the story if you're part Roma," she said. It was a standard childhood tale. The Indian goddess Parvati, impressed with an eleventh-century king's courage in battle, rewarded him with three sacred possessions—a necklace, a dagger, and crown. Combined, these treasures gave the Roma king the power to rule the world.

But then a hot-headed prince rose to the throne, lusted after a forbidden virgin, and misused those powers to take her. Heartbroken and disgraced, the woman cursed the Roma king and condemned the Gypsies to roam.

Soon afterward, the Roma were driven out of India, their priceless treasures lost. Generations of archeologists and fortune hunters had searched for the treasures ever since.

Logan shifted, made a low, rough sound of disgust. "Yeah, I've heard of it. Who hasn't? That necklace was in the news for months."

Dara nodded. The discovery of the necklace in a Spanish bank vault had rocked the world—and not just because it was Nazi war loot. It was proof that the treasures existed, that the legend had a kernel of truth. And when the Spanish government decided to return the necklace to its rightful owners—the Gypsies—experts from around the world had converged on the palace to get a closer look.

She'd been there that fateful night. She'd stood behind her parents as they waited to receive the necklace—and watched them die.

The memory surged, catching her unprepared, and she clutched the gelding's neck. She closed her eyes, struggled to ward off the inevitable parade of images—their splattered flesh, their pooling blood, her mother's vacant eyes.

She swallowed hard, battled the nausea rising in her throat, tried to push the horror aside. She'd had three months to come to grips with her parents' murders. Three months of flashbacks, nightmares, grappling to find logic in two tragic, pointless deaths.

She opened her eyes, dragged her gaze to the unyielding man beside the horse. "I don't know where the crown is," she said quietly. "No one does. But the dagger is here in Peru. I've studied documents from the time of Pizarro, the *conquistadores*. And about two months ago, I figured out where it is."

"In Quillacocha." His voice was flat.

"Yes, in the royal tomb." She tightened her grip on her pack—the backpack that contained her research, the diagrams of the tomb, proof in case anything happened to her. "I'm sure it's the Roma dagger. The description fits it exactly—the patterned wootz steel they used in India at the time, the gold hilt inlaid with amber, the engravings of the sun and moon. And once we get to Quillacocha, I know exactly where to look."

"The only place you're going is the first town over the pass. You can get a bus to Cusco, and then a flight to Lima from there."

"But—"

"Forget it." His eyes turned fierce, and her heart beat fast. "There's no way I'll take you to Quillacocha. It's going to be dangerous enough trying to cross that pass. I'll be damned if I'll risk your life—or mine—for a chunk of gold."

"I'm not going to keep it." Even the idea shocked her. The dagger was a symbol for the Roma people, an artifact steeped in legend, history. A treasure so ancient, so powerful, that a secret society was slaughtering her people to find it. *Their* people, since Logan was Roma, too.

"I'll hand it over to the authorities as soon as I get it," she said. "My colleague's taking care of the permits now."

He shook his head. "I don't care what you plan to do with it. It's still not worth your life or mine."

He was wrong. She was her people's leader. She had a duty to keep them safe—even if it cost her life.

"I don't have much choice," she said, subdued now. "I have to find it."

"There's always a choice."

Not for her. She tilted her head up to meet his gaze. "Either way, I intend to find it. The Roma need that blade. It will get them pride, hope for a better future, for justice."

"Justice?" He let out a bitter sound. "If you believe that, then you're a fool." He leaned toward her, and the sudden anger in his gaze made her want to step back. "No one cares about justice. Not for the Roma, not anyone. In this world, only the strong survive—and they look out for themselves."

She stared at him, appalled by his cynicism, at the bitterness tingeing his voice. "But…that's not true. How can you say that? You care. You help the miners. You haul their silver and gold."

"That's my job. I'm not doing it to be nice."

"I don't believe that." He risked his life to carry that gold. And he'd returned to the bar to save her.

"Believe it."

"But—"

"I'm not a hero," he warned, his voice so fierce she stepped back. "So don't make me into one. I live alone, work alone, and I don't get involved. Not with you, not anyone. Not for anything."

His words lashed at her, his fury underscored with something starker, something that sounded like pain. He turned his broad back to her and stalked away, leading his gelding to a rocky ridge.

Her stomach churned as she watched him go, at the darkness she'd heard in his voice. She knew all about pain, about guilt. She lived with the terrible irony that her parents—the beloved royal couple, respected and revered by their people—had died while she, the one not worthy to lead, had survived.

But unlike Logan, she didn't have the luxury of withdrawing into the wilderness and living alone. She had a duty, a responsibility to her people. And they desperately needed her help.

She followed him along the rocky trail to the outcrop, then stopped a short distance behind. She studied the set to his powerful shoulders, the tension in his rigid stance.

And she knew that even if he refused to help her, she owed this man an apology. Whatever had happened to him in the past, whatever had driven him to this lonely exile, he didn't deserve more grief.

Thunder rattled the earth again, making the gelding prance, and the sky turned darker yet. She shivered, moved closer to Logan, tried to figure out what to say.

"I'm sorry," she said at last, her voice subdued. "I couldn't tell you about the dagger at first because I didn't know if I could trust you. I didn't mean to hurt anyone. Not you, not the miners. I didn't know they'd have to go without their supplies.

"If you don't want to help me, I understand." Her voice quivered, her throat closed up at the thought of hiking these mountains alone. Even in the few hours she'd spent with him, Logan had made her feel safe. "But I have to find that dagger. I can't give up."

She stepped beside him, placed her fingers on his iron bicep. He flinched, and she dropped her hand. "If you won't take me there…" Her stomach lurched, and she sucked in a breath. "Could you at least draw me a map, tell me where it is?"

He turned around then. His hard gaze clamped on hers, and her pulse sped into her throat. He moved close, so close she inhaled his potent heat, felt the sexual pull of his mouth. "There's only one problem with your story, darlin'."

"What?" she breathed.

"You've got a sniper on your trail."

"A sniper?" Shock rippled through her. "Are you sure?"

"I know what I saw."

Her head felt light. A stark chill crept up her back. She'd hoped, prayed, that it was only an antiquities hunter on her heels, a rival archeologist who'd gotten wind of her find. But a trained killer...that could only mean... She shivered, suddenly shaky, and pressed her trembling hand to her lips.

"I've seen plenty of archeologists in these hills," he continued, and his hard gaze drove into hers. "Treasure hunters, drug smugglers, revolutionaries. But that man's a pro. And he's hunting you."

"He's not..." Her voice faltered, but it was pointless to evade the truth. Logan deserved to know what they were up against. She'd forced him into this mess.

"I think he's a member of that secret society, the Order of the Black Crescent Moon."

Logan didn't move. His eyes stayed locked on hers. The wind gusted again, lashing them with freezing rain, but she ignored the drops, the cold. "You've heard of them?"

"Yeah, I've heard of them. They even made the news out here."

She chewed her lip, prayed that he hadn't seen a picture of her or heard her name. Because if he realized that she was the Roma princess, he'd never take her to that tomb. Traveling through the wilderness with an archeologist was one thing, being alone with the princess taboo. And she desperately needed his help.

"A few weeks ago, a member of the society broke into my apartment and tried to find my notes about the dagger," she admitted. And murdered her bodyguard. She shuddered at the gruesome memory, at the horror of another senseless death, that there could be a society so inhuman, so cruel that they'd slaughter innocents to reach their goal. "And I think…that sniper could be one of them."

His gaze burned into hers, so intent that she couldn't breathe. And then he turned, faced the ravine, and she dragged in an unsteady breath.

She eyed the unyielding set to his muscular back, the huge hand fisting the reins, and her throat squeezed shut. She couldn't blame him for being furious. She'd put him at a terrible risk.

"So this man knows you have the information." His voice was stripped of any emotion.

"Yes." She tightened her grip on her bag, the diagrams and translations they'd killed her bodyguard to find.

"He'll come after you, then. He won't give up. No matter where I take you, he's going to follow. If I leave you, he's going to attack."

She didn't answer. They both knew it was true.

The cold wind moaned through the rocky canyon. Thunder rumbled closer, and the gelding bobbed his head.

"Why me?" Logan whipped around, and she took a quick step back. "Damn it all. Why did you have to choose me?"

She trembled at the darkness in his eyes, the turmoil straining his voice. "I told you. My colleague recommended you. Pedro Hernandez. He teaches at the University of California."

"I've never heard of him."

"But he knows you. Or knows of you, your reputation with the trails."

He gripped his neck, then slashed down his hand, made a frustrated sound in his throat. He didn't want to help her; she understood that. And it wasn't only due to the danger, because she doubted that this man feared much.

No, something more was bothering him. Beneath that cynicism and anger roiled feelings as stark as the granite framing the sky.

"I'm sorry," she repeated, her voice ragged. Her stomach

swirled with resignation and dread. "I really am. But I don't have a choice. I have to get that dagger, whether you help me or not."

He looked away, his strong jaw taut. The wind keened through the canyon like a defeated cry.

And then his eyes met hers, and he looked caged, trapped. "It looks like you'll get your wish." The empty finality in his voice made her heart squeeze. "We'll head for Quillacocha."

"I...thank you."

He shook his head, his expression so bleak that her chest ached. "Don't thank me. You know what they say about being careful what you wish for." He nodded toward the jagged peaks behind him. "Quillacocha's that way."

Her gaze followed the dirt trail as it crisscrossed the mountain and then stopped abruptly at some ancient stone steps. The staircase wound steeply upward for what looked like miles, then disappeared into the mist.

"My gelding can't take those steps. You either hike it alone and meet me on the other side, or you ride with me."

She scanned the sheer, exposed face of the mountain, and a wild sound rose in her throat. She didn't need him to spell it out. If the horse faltered, took a misstep, they'd have a long, deadly distance to fall.

"The sniper—"

"I don't know where he is," he admitted. "He might have lost our tracks when we crossed the creek, but I can't be sure."

She labored to breathe and pressed her suddenly clammy palms to her thighs. If that sniper was close, and they were on that open slope...

Her eyes met his. She'd dragged Logan into this mess. She'd stick with him, no matter what the price. "I'll ride."

He nodded, mounted the gelding, and his desolate eyes locked on hers. "But if you're the type to pray, darlin', this would be a real good time to start."

* * *

Whatever anxiety Dara had suffered on that rope suspension bridge was nothing compared to riding across an open slope in a sniper's sight.

She huddled against Logan's back, her throat clamped tight, goose bumps chasing over her skin. The storm had crept closer, lower as they veered off the trail at the impassable stone steps, then switched back across the steep hill. The cold wind buffeted her face with violent gusts. Thunder rumbled in the distance.

She eyed the mist-shrouded peaks above them, struggling to stay calm. She knew Logan was riding as fast as he dared, trying to get them to safety before the storm broke—and before that sniper attacked.

Lightning flashed, making her heart jump. Thunder boomed, and the gelding flicked his ears back and pranced. Dara shifted even closer to Logan's back, taking comfort in his warmth, his strength, the expert way he scanned the terrain.

But that expertise came at a price. The man never smiled, never relaxed. There was a stark sense of loneliness about him, an aura of desolation and grief. And she longed to know more about him, where he came from, what pain had driven him to this lonely exile—and why he denied that he cared.

The storm drummed again, making her aching forehead throb, and then a sharp crack split the air. Logan flinched, slumped forward over the gelding's neck, and Dara's heart vaulted into her throat.

He'd been shot!

"Logan," she cried.

"Hold on," he shouted over his shoulder as the horse tossed his head back and reared. She clung to Logan's shirt, struggled not to lose her grip, but the horse reared up even more. The shirt ripped from her hands, and she gasped.

The horse dropped down and bolted forward, but Dara's

momentum pulled her back. She fell off the horse, slammed to the dirt with a muffled cry, her breath jarred from her lungs.

She didn't stop. The hill was steep, slick from the gusting rain, and she continued careening downward, smashing through bushes, dislodging rocks. She clutched at branches, wet grass, trying desperately to stop, but just skidded and rolled down the slope.

She crashed to a stop seconds later in a clump of grass. She lay still, rasping painfully for air. Her head throbbed. Her ribs and shoulders ached. Dirt was ground into her mouth.

She wiped her mouth on her sleeve, stretched cautiously to probe for injuries, then eased out an uneven breath. Nothing was broken, thank God.

But Logan had been shot.

Her heart leaped in a surge of panic, and she quickly lifted her head. But then she froze. *The sniper.* He was still out there. She pressed herself flat to the ground.

She squeezed in a breath, ignored the pebbles digging into her cheek, listened for signs of pursuit. But there were no more shots, no hoofbeats, only the wind whipping past, the rumble of the oncoming storm.

She trembled in the eerie quiet, crushed down the slithering fear. She'd fallen down the steep, grassy part of the slope, landing near the eroded edge of a cliff. The rain was picking up, soaking her shirt and turning the grass slick, but she could probably work her way back up.

Except for the sniper.

Her breath caught, but she eased it back out, fought the dread slinking deep in her gut. She could do this. She wasn't defenseless. And she had a gun. She inched her arm to the side, reached for her pack, but it was gone.

Her heart stopped. Panic swarmed through her nerves. Her gun. *The files.* She inched up her head, spotted the backpack snagged on a bush several yards away beyond the eroded edge of the cliff.

She drew in air, fought for calm. Okay. Okay. She could still do this. She just had to scoot out and grab the pack, then work her way up the cliff.

Her heart rapping hard against her rib cage, she snaked along the ground toward the edge. She ignored the ache in her back, the pain bludgeoning her head, forced herself to slide slowly, slowly through the loose stones and dirt.

A foot from the crumbling edge, she stopped. She eyed the canyon yawning hundreds of feet below, the jagged boulders on the distant ground. A fall would lead to certain death.

She inched out a trembling hand, but she couldn't reach the pack. It was too low, stuck on a bush growing under the edge.

She tugged in a ragged breath, battled down the panic bleeding her skin of warmth. If a bush was growing on the cliff, the ground couldn't be too unstable. And she needed that gun, those files.

She crawled closer to the edge, inhaled for courage, forced thoughts of the void from her mind. She stretched, stretched again, then lunged and grasped the strap. *Got it.* She released her breath.

And then the cliff gave way.

She shrieked, plummeted in a jumble of earth and rocks into empty space. Her arms flailed. Terror blanked out her mind. And then she slammed to a halt against a rock.

She moaned, struggled to suck in air, but it was agony to breathe. Her head ached. Her back and ribs burned. Dirt rained on her face, and she coughed. She closed her eyes, and groaned.

So where had she landed now? Not the bottom of the canyon if she was still alive. She wheezed again, tried to draw air past the vise constricting her chest. Careful not to move too fast, she rolled her head to the side.

And froze. Inches from her face the ground vanished.

She'd landed on a narrow ledge.

Oh, God.

She didn't move. She lay petrified, every muscle cemented in place. Only her heart wobbled to life, making a feeble throb in her chest.

She slashed her gaze to the cliff behind her, scanned the sheer, high stretch of rock—too steep to climb.

A dull clanging rose in her skull. Nausea churned through her gut. She was stranded, with no way up. No way down.

Thunder boomed, rattling the ledge, and she wheezed in a reedy breath. The ledge was unstable. Any movement, even shifting her weight, could cause it to collapse.

And Logan couldn't help her. He'd been injured, shot. And that sniper was nearby, stalking them, drawing closer, closer…

Hysteria bubbled inside her. A chilly sweat beaded her face. She closed her eyes, fought back the panic clawing her chest, the urge to shriek, to cry, to scream.

Logan hadn't been kidding about saying prayers.

Chapter 6

He'd failed again. He'd exposed Dara to danger, and now she was lost, maybe injured.

Maybe dead.

Dread pounded through him as he crept back around the hill. He scanned the deserted hillside, the steep slope that plummeted to the rocky gorge. Lightning crackled in the darkened sky, and he tightened his grip on the reins to control his skittish horse.

He knew he was lucky to be alive. If Rupper hadn't jumped at the sound of thunder, that bullet would have blasted his skull.

But Dara...

His stomach muscles clenched, but he forced himself to breathe. He'd find her. He had to find her. No matter what else happened, he'd make damned sure this woman survived.

The wind gusted again, whipping him with icy rain, but he

ignored the rain, ignored the blood dripping through the beard stubble on his jaw, scanned the trail of flattened grass that angled down the slope. It ended abruptly at the eroded cliff.

His heart plunged. Oh, hell. She'd fallen off the cliff.

"Dara!" he called. He waited a beat, his urgency rising. "Dara!" he shouted again.

"I'm here. Down here," she called back in a shaky voice.

He eased out his pent-up breath, forced his rigid shoulders to relax. She'd survived. And she didn't sound far down the cliff. "Are you all right? Can you move?"

"I'm…fine, but I'm on a ledge and I…I don't think it's going to hold."

Her voice rose at the end, trembled hard, and his heart accelerated again. He had to keep her calm, get her off the ledge before the unstable earth collapsed.

But where was the sniper?

He swore, sent an uneasy glance at their back trail, his need to save Dara warring with common sense. He had to find out where that sniper was—before the man caught up and shot them dead.

"Hold on," he urged her. "I'll be right back with a rope. Don't move."

"I'll be here."

They both hoped.

He shook his head, amazed that she sounded so calm. He'd expected her to be hysterical by now.

He pumped a round into his assault rifle, then crept around the hill with his back to the rocks, and scanned the open slope. His gaze settled on a cluster of trees nearly a mile downhill. The sniper had to be hiding there. It was the only cover around.

But how had he caught up so fast? They'd had a good lead on him back at the bridge.

A shiver licked down his spine, a trickle of sudden awareness. This man was an expert tracker, as good as Logan himself.

And he was familiar enough with these mountains to hang back and take his time.

Logan wouldn't underestimate him again.

He waited for several more heartbeats, watched the trees through the slanting rain. Nothing moved. He'd have to risk it.

He sprinted back to the horse, jammed the rifle into his pack, and grabbed the rope. They had twenty minutes, tops, before that sniper ventured from those trees and got them within range again.

Which meant he had to work fast.

He secured one end of the rope through the pommel, tugged it to make sure it would hold. "I'm throwing the rope down now," he called to Dara. He swung the rope, tossed the end down the slope, sent it sliding over the edge.

"I see it," Dara called back a second later.

"Can you reach it?"

"I don't know. I need to stand up."

More thunder rolled. Rupper pinned his ears back and bunched his neck. "Easy, Rupe," he murmured. The last thing he needed was for the horse to bolt.

"I can't reach it." Dara's voice was tight. "Can you get it any closer?"

He scanned the slope but knew it would never work. The hill was too steep to move the horse lower. And he needed the gelding to anchor the rope in case he slipped.

"That's as far as it goes. Are you sure you can't reach it?"

"I…maybe. If I jump."

Jump? "How wide is the ledge?"

"Not wide." Her voice quivered, and he knew what she hadn't said. If she jumped and missed…

He wished he could do it for her, wished he could find a different way to bring her up. But there was no other option, no time.

He tugged on his leather work gloves, lowered himself to

the ground and braced his feet against a rock. He ignored the blood trickling down his face, the rain dripping off his hat, and grabbed the rope.

"All right, darlin', I'm ready when you are." He steeled himself, pulled in a breath. "When you grab the rope, just hang on, and I'll pull you up."

"Logan, I…I have to tell you about the dagger…in case I don't—"

"You'll make it," he said, his voice rough. He refused to let her have any doubts. He wouldn't—couldn't—fail again. "Just grab the rope and hold on."

"Right. Right. Okay." Her voice shook hard. "Here I go."

His adrenaline surged. Every cell in his body tensed. A second later, the rope jerked tight.

"Hold on!" he shouted and started to pull.

He hauled it in, hard, hand over hand, knowing she couldn't hang on long. His shoulders strained. His breath came in uneven rasps. His biceps trembled and burned. But he ignored the pain, blinked back the sweat stinging his eyes, focused on hauling the rope up the slope. *Faster, faster.*

And then the rope stopped. It was stuck. He shook the sweat from his eyes, jerked hard to dislodge the rope, and Dara shrieked. "Logan, stop!"

His hands stilled. "What's wrong?"

"I'm caught on the rocks. Under the ledge. Oh, God."

Panic leached through her voice, making his heart drum. "Push off from the cliff with your feet."

"I'll…try…"

Thunder sounded again, vibrating the earth. Behind him, the gelding reared.

Oh, hell. "Whoa!" he yelled as the gelding pulled the rope tight. "Rupper, whoa!" The horse reared again, and his panic rose.

He leaped up, hauled back hard on the rope, desperate to

keep Rupper still. He planted his feet, angled his weight, but the gelding rolled his eyes back and pulled.

Damn. Damn! He had to stop him. If the horse bolted now, he'd knock Dara off her end.

But how could he stop the horse?

Grunting, using every ounce of strength he had, he battled to keep the rope in place. His back muscles cramped. The veins stood out on his arms. But the horse only thrashed and jerked back.

He had to cut him loose.

Moving quickly, Logan stooped, let go of the rope with one hand and yanked the knife from his boot. But the horse twisted back, sending pain scorching through his arm, and dragged him over the ground.

Dara screamed.

"Hold on!" he shouted and struggled to stop the horse. His shoulder flamed. Sweat streamed into his eyes. He dug in his heels, slashed at the rope, fought to keep Dara from slamming against the rocks.

He sawed with the knife, ignoring the burn in his arm, the fierce spasms mauling his back. And then the rope snapped free. The horse bolted off. Logan dropped the knife, grabbed the sliced end of the rope with both hands and pulled.

"Push off," he yelled as he struggled to hold her. His vision hazed. His left arm trembled and pulsed. *Damn.* He'd wrenched that shoulder bad.

"Hurry," Dara cried, her voice shaking hard now. And he knew she was close to the end.

He pulled, then pulled again. Her head inched into view. He worked faster, harder. She slammed against the cliff and groaned.

"Don't let go," he urged her. He saw the pain grooving her face, the flush darkening her skin, the effort it was taking her to hold on. The fear that she wouldn't last swelled.

"Hang on, Dara," he ground out. "You can do it. Just a few yards more."

She managed to work her feet over the ledge, and then he dragged her up the hill, ignoring his own pain as she scraped and bumped over the rocks.

"Almost there. Come on, darlin'." He gave one final heave, and then she was next to him, close enough for him to grab her arm. He reached down with his good arm and hauled her up, and she collapsed on him in the dirt.

He couldn't move. He just sat there, cradling her in his lap, sawing at air. His heart still raced. His back muscles spasmed and burned. His biceps jumped from fatigue.

But he wrapped his good arm around her and absorbed the warmth of her body, the frantic beat of her pulse, thankful she had survived.

Because that had been too damned close.

He lifted his hand, ignoring the pain wracking his injured shoulder, and smoothed back her loose strands of hair. Shivers ran through her slender frame, and he pulled her closer, needing to make sure she was really okay.

"You can let go of the rope," he finally murmured into her hair, his fear for her deepening his voice.

"Oh, right." She hitched out a shaky laugh. She lifted her head, pried her fingers from the rope, gave him a tremulous smile.

"Are you okay?" Her face was covered with dirt, streaked by rain.

"Yes. I just—" her full lips quivered "—really, really hate heights." Her breath made a little catch, and he realized just how terrified she'd been.

He put his gloved hand under her chin, traced the line of her throat with his thumb. A raw scrape marred one cheek, a bruise swelled under her eye. She was battered, wet. She'd been shot at, dragged up a cliff, had almost died.

And yet, she hadn't complained.

His admiration swelled. No matter how misguided her idealism, no matter how foolhardy her desire to find that fabled blade, he couldn't help but respect her strength. She'd ventured into the wilderness alone, battled her way across that suspension bridge, scraped her way back up the cliff.

She was brave, beautiful. He took in the curve of her cheeks, the long dark lashes fringing those exotic eyes, and his heart struck an uneven beat. Even beneath the grime, her skin gleamed with the promise of sweetness, tugging at something forgotten inside him, something he'd thought was long dead.

But then she gasped. "Logan, your cheek! You've been shot."

"It's just a graze."

But she put her hand on his jaw, leaned closer to inspect his face. And he inhaled the heat of her skin, felt her round breasts stroking his chest, her soft hands petting his face.

"We need to stop the bleeding," she said and moved closer yet.

The movement caressed his groin, and he sucked in his breath. She stilled at the sound, and her eyes met his. Her soft, erotic eyes.

His heartbeat slowed, thumped into his skull. And that awareness, that heat, quivered between them again.

Her gaze dropped to his mouth, slid back up. She touched her tongue to her lips.

And hunger prowled through him, a deep, pulling drag of desire. His blood ran hot. His entire body clenched.

He wanted her. Damn, how he wanted her.

He breathed through his mouth, tried to quell the primitive rush of lust. But it didn't do any good. He wanted to touch her, taste her, feel her over him, under him—take her any and every way he could.

But it was more than lust, more than heat. Something deeper stirred inside him, something more profound. The need to defend, to protect.

To possess.

He stilled, shocked. He couldn't get involved with this woman. With any woman. Not now, not later. Plus, there was a sniper behind them. In seconds they both could be dead.

"Later," he ground out, and she blinked. "The first aid can wait. We've got to move."

"Right." She lurched to her feet, her movements stiff.

He bit back his own groan and rose, then waited until the dizziness passed. His shoulder throbbed. A deep ache pulsed through his arm.

"Are you all right?" Dara asked.

"Yeah," he lied. "Everything's great." His shooting arm was wrenched. A sniper wanted them dead.

And he'd nearly lost his sanity and kissed her—again.

He settled his hat on his head, retrieved his knife, the rope, stalked to where the gelding had stopped. Wanting Dara was one thing. He could handle sex, keep the physical needs in their place. But no way could he let himself care about her, let her worm herself under his skin.

He reached for the saddle, hissed at the fierce pain scaring his arm, reminded himself of his rules. Stay detached. Don't get involved.

Don't care.

Right. He swung himself into the saddle, glanced down at the courageous woman hobbling toward him. And had a bad feeling that it was already too late.

Chapter 7

Something was wrong.

Dara could feel the tension rippling off Logan's back, the wariness in the way he kept checking behind them as they climbed up the mountain through the storm. Whatever he saw through the encroaching darkness had him worried, on edge, as charged as the lightning crackling through the ominous sky.

She shivered, her own nerves adding to the chill as they rode up to a crude tunnel chiseled from the mountain, and stopped.

"We'll rest here for a minute," he announced.

Only a minute? She slid off the gelding and stifled a moan. They'd been riding for hours, heading endlessly upward on a convoluted path through the gusting rain, and she was hungry, exhausted, soaked. Her body ached. Her head felt as if a demon were caged inside and bludgeoning his way back out.

She stumbled into the primitive tunnel, wiped her dripping

face on her sleeve, and waited for Logan to dismount. Lightning sizzled in the menacing sky. Thunder vibrated the ground.

"Isn't it dangerous to keep riding in the lightning?" she asked as he led the gelding into the narrow space.

"It's riskier not to." He stopped beside her, the lines in his grim face stark. "The rain's giving us an edge, helping wipe out our tracks."

Then why did he look so tense? "You think the sniper's still close?"

He nodded, and water dripped off his hat. "I saw him. He's about ninety minutes back. We've put some distance between us, but not enough. He's too damned good."

She glanced uneasily out the tunnel at the encroaching darkness. The strong wind slashed at the grass. Black clouds obliterated the sky.

Her heart accelerated, punched into her throat. "Maybe we should keep riding," she said, struggling to keep her voice calm.

"We can spare a few minutes to rest. It'll be our last chance for a while." He opened one of Rupper's packs, handed her his canteen.

"Thanks." She gripped the plastic bottle, unscrewed the cap and drank, letting the cool water soothe her parched throat. But she couldn't stop the terrible anxiety creeping through her. What wasn't Logan saying? What had put that troubled look in his eyes? He hadn't looked this tense before.

"How do you feel?" he asked, and caught her eye.

"All right," she answered cautiously, even though every inch of her body ached. "Why?"

Lightning flashed, turning the angles of his face harsh. His dark eyes stayed locked on hers. "We have to make a choice. We can continue on this path or take a shortcut. But the shortcut goes straight up."

Straight up? Her jaw sagged. She'd thought the path they were on was steep.

But Logan wouldn't suggest a harder route if it weren't urgent.

She shoved the wet strands of hair from her face, fought back the uneasiness pitching her gut. "You think we'll lose him if we take the shortcut?"

"Maybe." His frown deepened. "He won't expect it. By the time he figures out that he's lost us and backtracks, the rain should have washed out our tracks."

She felt the fatigue wracking her limbs, the fierce ache hammering her head, and stifled a sigh. "So we go up."

"It's a hell of a hike," he warned, his voice low. "The trail's narrow, steep, washed away in spots. We'll have to walk most of the way. And it will be slippery in the rain, hard to see in the dark."

Dangerous. Dread trickled through her. Her mind flashed back to that ledge, and an awful jolt of panic buzzed through her skull. But this wasn't the time to be weak. "I can do it."

"You're sure?"

"Yes." She'd make sure of it. She handed him back the canteen.

His eyes studied hers for several seconds. And then he nodded, turned back to the pack, stuck the canteen inside. She caught his wince as he moved.

"What's wrong? Are you hurt?" He'd been favoring that arm since he'd pulled her off the cliff.

"I just pulled a muscle. Some horse liniment will loosen it up." He rifled through the pack, handed her a bottle of gel.

"What about your cheek?" Even in the dim light the scrape looked raw.

"We'll take care of it later, when the rain stops. There's not much point until then." He removed his hat, unbuttoned his flannel shirt and tugged it off.

She unscrewed the cap from the bottle of liniment and

sniffed, expecting something foul, but it had a pleasant, herbal scent. "Kneel down, and I'll rub it in."

"You don't mind?"

"No, of course not." It was the least she could do after he'd saved her life.

He grabbed the back of his T-shirt by the neck, stripped it off one-handed, and her breath wedged in her throat. His shoulders were broad, ridged with powerful muscles. Huge biceps bulged in his arms. The flickering light made his black hair gleam, turned his skin a molten bronze.

He tested his shoulder, grimaced, then lowered himself to his knees. She opened the bottle, tried not to gawk at his gorgeous muscles, but she couldn't help it. She'd never seen a more beautifully sculpted man.

No wonder he'd been able to pull her off that cliff.

She knelt beside him on the rocky ground, squirted gel on her trembling palm. She shouldn't gape, shouldn't think of this as sexual, she scolded herself, even if the man was half-naked. She was only helping him out, caring for his wounds, just as he'd rescued her.

If only she could convince her body of that. She slathered the gel on his shoulder, tried not to notice the heat of his skin, the sleek, roped muscles under her palm, his intriguing male scent permeating the air.

Her gaze drifted to his handsome profile, those straight, black brows, the sexy beard stubble coating his neck. His back muscles flexed, and she pulled her gaze past his rippled abs, to the worn jeans molding his thighs.

And every enthralling bit of him in between.

She cleared her suddenly parched throat. "I never thanked you for saving me when I fell."

"You were lucky you landed on that ledge."

"I know." Her belly tightened at the memory. "But if you

hadn't pulled me up…" She shuddered, trying not to remember the sickening fear, the terror when she'd had to jump. Because if she'd missed…

He turned his head, and his dark eyes pinned hers. "I told you these mountains were dangerous. You could have been killed back there. What if I hadn't gotten to you in time?"

The anger in his voice took her aback. Did he feel responsible for that? "It wasn't your fault I fell off the horse," she argued. She squeezed more liniment into her palm, worked it into the tight muscles bunching his back. "And no place is completely safe. Accidents can happen anytime, anywhere."

So could murder. The secret society had shot her parents in a crowded palace ballroom with armed guards all around.

And now that same society was stalking her.

Her hands trembled. Thunder rattled through the tunnel like an ominous warning, making the nerves along her belly churn. But she forced her thoughts from her stalker, the fear, and focused on massaging the liniment into Logan's warm back, kneading the tension from his knotted tendons, absorbing the heat of his skin. Taking comfort in his courage, his nearness, his strength.

He was so tough, so stoic. So bleak. And she wondered again what had driven him to this lonely lifestyle, what had made him so cynical about life.

She hesitated, wanting to know more about him, not sure how to ask. She poured more gel into her palm, resumed the massage. "Your accent sounds American," she finally said.

"Texas." His deep voice rasped in the quiet air. He shifted closer, and she forgot to breathe. Did he have any idea how intimate this felt, kneeling close to him in the shadowy light, how badly he disrupted her thoughts?

She cleared her throat, forced air to her lungs, tried not to inhale his seductive scent. "And your mother was Roma?"

She thought at first he wouldn't answer. Long seconds passed in silence. Wind keened through the tunnel and chilled her skin. But then he let out a weary sound.

"Yeah, she was Roma. She got pregnant by a drifting cowhand, and her clan threw her out. They said she was *marime,* polluted, and she got shunned."

Shunned. Shock rippled through her, and she paused. Whatever she'd expected him to say, it wasn't that. Being cast out, condemned to live in the non-Roma world, was the most severe penalty the Roma had—equal to death.

And Logan... Her heart faltered. What an awful burden for him to bear.

"I'm sorry," she said, struggling for something to say. "I know it seems severe. Unfair. People can be...rigid. The Roma..." She shrugged, unable to defend the practice, not sure how to explain. "The culture's ancient, with old beliefs, old rules. The rules protect them, keep outsiders away. But it also means that change comes slowly." If at all.

And a princess had even less freedom, was held to an even stricter standard than most. Everything she did was scrutinized—what she wore, what she said, who she talked to and where she went.

And Dara had never measured up. Her people considered her rebellious. Her mother had butted heads with her, trying to make her conform. And her father... Her father had simply sighed, saddened by a daughter he couldn't understand, a princess not worthy to lead.

But she couldn't tell Logan that. "So how did you end up in Peru?" she asked instead.

"My father thought he could strike it rich mining gold."

She poured more liniment into her hand, stroked his powerful bicep, massaged the taut ridges beneath his warm skin. "I take it that didn't happen."

"Hardly." The grooves tightened around his mouth. "He got killed in a bar fight about a month after we arrived."

"But you stayed?"

"There was no place else to go. My mother's family wouldn't take us back. So she got a job as a maid on a hacienda. I cleaned stalls, helped on the trails until she got sick. Then I went into the mines."

"You were a miner?" He'd worked in those awful conditions? Her hand stilled on his arm, and her eyes met his. "But…how old were you?"

"Thirteen. I was smaller then, skinnier, but I still barely fit down those shafts. I spent the whole damned summer living in those tunnels, nearly killed myself blasting out ore. But I finally scraped out some gold to buy some medicine for my mom."

"Was it enough?"

He let out a bitter laugh. "Hell if I know. I got robbed on my way down the mountain. And by the time I dug more gold, my mother was dead."

She stared at him, stunned at the guilt in his voice, the self-disgust. "You can't possibly blame yourself. You did everything you could." And more.

"I trusted the men who robbed me, walked right into their trap. I was a fool."

"You were a child." A child trying desperately to do a man's job, to save his sick mother, his only connection in a hostile world.

"Yeah, I was a child, all right." His gaze held hers. "But nothing's changed. This is a dangerous place, Dara, too dangerous. You don't have any business being out here."

He was wrong. But she understood his pain, his guilt. She gazed at his rugged face, his tormented eyes, and her heart stumbled. She reached out and stroked his bristled jaw. "It's not easy to lose people you love," she whispered. "My family's dead, too. And I'd have done anything to save their lives."

His eyes held hers. And for several heartbeats neither spoke. Lightning flickered on the chiseled walls. The gelding stamped his hooves. And an understanding curled between them, a connection.

And something more.

Something far more primal.

Her gaze dropped to his sleek, muscled chest gleaming in the erratic light, then stalled on his masculine mouth. Quivers rose in her belly, shimmered over her nerves. She brushed her hand up his stubbled jaw, felt those desperado whiskers under her palm—coarse, thrilling. Arousing.

Their gazes locked. Her heart abruptly lost its beat.

"Logan," she whispered, and her voice shook.

He rose, pulling her up with him, his hot, dark eyes latched on hers. Lightning flashed, putting the harsh angles of his face in sharp relief. Hunger burned in his eyes.

"Do you have any idea what you're doing to me?" His deep voice rumbled through her nerves.

She trembled, wanting so badly to kiss him that she couldn't breathe. "I think…It's the same thing you're doing to me."

He placed his big, callused hand on her neck, making her heart thud fast. His dark eyes riveted hers.

And then he pulled her against him. And she gloried in the feel of his tough, muscled thighs, the hard bulge of his massive arms.

Then he slanted his mouth over hers in a deep, smoldering kiss that blasted away every thought. Excitement jolted through her. She slipped her hands up his back, felt his muscles flex under her palms, feeling his power, his strength.

He slid his hand to her jaw, changed the angle of the kiss, and her pulse went wild. A fever scalded through her, a deep drugging heat that thickened her blood. Her senses whirled. Her body throbbed. She wanted, needed more.

His mouth trailed along her jaw, her neck, sending sensual currents rippling and skipping down her skin. He ran his big hands over her hips, tugged her tightly against him. Pleasure shocked through her, and she gasped.

Stunned, bombarded with the delirious sensations, she gave herself over, let her head fall back, surrendered to the shattering ache. She couldn't stop. She never wanted to stop. Pleasure coiled inside her, so fierce that she wanted to burst.

But he pulled back, lifted his head. His fingers dug into her hips. She inched up her hands, stroked the stark grooves framing his mouth, met the dark eyes blazing at hers.

He hissed. "I'm trying to do the right thing here. If you don't want where this is heading, you'd better stop sending me signals."

She stilled, blinked, struggled to order her chaotic thoughts. A lifetime of rules had crumbled beneath his sensual onslaught. Nothing had ever felt as thrilling, as exciting, as being in Logan's arms.

But he was right. The Roma had rules—strict rules—and she was breaking a huge taboo. Uncertain suddenly, she lowered her hands.

He swore, set her away, putting some distance between them. "We've got to go," he said, sounding angry now. He turned, picked up his shirt, struggled to pull it on.

Confused by his shift in mood, she moved to help. "Here, let me—"

"It's better if you don't touch me right now." The fury in his voice made her hands freeze.

Even more uncertain now, she watched him, and a sick feeling churned through her gut. That kiss had thrilled her, devastated her. Remnants of pleasure still shocked through her blood. And she'd felt his answering hunger, his need. So why was he angry now?

He shot her a scowl from beside the horse. "Do you have any rain gear?"

"No." She folded her arms under her breasts, and her face turned hot. "Just this sweatshirt."

He opened his pack, rummaged through it, pulled a rain poncho out. "Put this on. It'll keep you dry."

She was already wet, but didn't argue. Still flushing, she took the plastic poncho and turned away, then pulled it over her head. She smoothed the huge garment over her knees, adjusted her backpack to keep it dry, struggled to figure out what had gone wrong.

He had wanted her. She was sure of that.

And he appealed to her in so many ways. He was tough, dangerous. Honorable and complex. The sexiest man she'd ever met.

And she liked that he didn't treat her like a princess. He didn't cater to her, didn't impose rules on her. He treated her like a woman, like a desirable woman, as if he wanted her for herself—not just because of who she was.

Of course, he didn't know who she really was.

But being with him was liberating, exciting. He gave her a long denied chance at freedom, a chance to simply be herself.

He pulled on a vest, his leather hat, favoring his injured arm. Then he led his gelding through the darkened tunnel, and she trailed him, stumbling over the uneven ground.

But she knew that he was right. He wasn't a man to toy with. He was virile, potent. And if she didn't want to go where those kisses were heading, she had to stop—stop looking at him, stop touching him, stop yearning for him.

But was that what she really wanted? It was what she *should* want. What a proper princess would want.

Too bad she'd never been proper.

They reached the end of the shadowy tunnel, and he turned to face her again. "You're sure you can handle that shortcut?"

She raised her chin to meet his gaze. "I'm sure."

He studied her for a moment, then nodded. "We'll push through the night. I'll lead. If you have a problem, call out." Still scowling, he handed her the rope he'd attached to the saddle. "Hold on to this in case you slip."

Without warning, he moved close and grasped her chin, and her heart started to sprint. Lightning flickered behind him. His dark eyes seared into hers.

And then he kissed her—a deep, rough kiss that wiped out every thought.

Then, just as abruptly, he stepped back, grabbed the gelding's reins, and turned into the turbulent night.

Shattered, her senses in total turmoil, she pulled the rain poncho closer around her face and stepped outside the sheltering rocks.

The wind whipped against her, slashing her with freezing rain, and jerked the breath from her lungs. She shivered, tightened her grip on the rope, determined to forget the kiss, forget the need sizzling her veins, and concentrate on what mattered most—surviving the night.

They had a sniper close behind them, lightning threatening to strike, a treacherous mountain to cross. She couldn't let her attention slip, couldn't risk causing another accident that could get them both killed.

She drew in her breath, prepared herself to face the danger ahead.

But as she stepped into the seething night, the feel of Logan's kiss still lashing her nerves, she feared that the real danger might be the temptation brewing inside herself.

Chapter 8

Nearly ten hours later, they still hadn't lost the sniper.

Incredulous, Logan stood in the pre-dawn darkness and stared at the opposite ridge. He waited, his disbelief mounting, until lightning streaked over the landscape again, bathing it in a bluish tinge. The ridge was empty.

But he'd seen him. That sniper was back there tailing them, flitting in and out of view like an elusive ghost.

A deep feeling of dread seeped through him, a foreboding he couldn't quite shake. They'd spent the night climbing through the gusting rain, scrambling up ancient footpaths, over trails so old, so worn away by centuries of disuse that few people knew they were there, apart from a handful of Quechua shamans.

He bunched the leather reins in his fist, and uneasiness prowled through his nerves. Who was this guy? How had he followed them in the rain?

And where in the hell was he now?

"What's…wrong?" Dara wheezed as she staggered to a stop beside the horse. She doubled over, propped her hands on her knees. "Is that…man gone?"

Still troubled, he turned his attention to the exhausted woman at his side. Wet strands of hair clung to her cheeks. Her shallow breath rasped in the air. She'd slowed drastically over the past few hours, stumbling and lagging behind the horse, and was clearly past her limits now.

He was impressed that she'd lasted this long. This altitude was a killer, even for him. His heart still pounded from the relentless climb. His muscles were getting weak, and breathing at this elevation was like trying to suck air through cement.

"I don't see him," he hedged, determined not to worry her more. "But we won't know for sure until it's light."

"Then we'd…better…keep going." She straightened, lurched forward, and he leaped toward her and caught her arm. She grabbed the saddle, sagged against the blowing horse. "I'm…fine," she gasped.

The hell she was. He'd pushed the pace, forced her to scale the sheer terrain without a rest, hour after grueling hour.

He was amazed she hadn't complained.

His wife would have complained. She disliked the mountains, hated camping even more.

He pushed away the memory of his dead wife, returned his gaze to the determined woman draped over his horse. He couldn't imagine Dara whining. She was too stubborn, too fearless.

Too appealing—even in her battered state. He eyed the thick, silky braid sweeping low on her back, the gentle slope of her cheeks. She'd removed the rain poncho, and her damp T-shirt gloved her ample breasts.

He jerked his mind off that track. He couldn't let his attention wander to that kiss. Not now, not with their survival at stake.

He cut his gaze to the ridge. The storm was moving off as dawn approached, the lightning receding to an occasional flash. Beyond the hills, the emerging sun smeared a bloodred glow through the sky.

But daylight meant danger, a chance for that sniper to get a bead on them and shoot—which meant they couldn't stop.

"We'll reach the pass in another hour or two," he told her. "There's a cave, the entrance to an old mine shaft on the other side where we can rest." Assuming they lost the sniper by then.

"All right." She straightened, massaged the bridge of her nose, and the familiar gesture made him pause. She'd been kneading her forehead a lot in the past few hours.

"Does your head hurt?"

"No, it's—" she shook her head, winced and closed her eyes "—fine."

Oh, hell. This was all they needed. If she had altitude sickness… "How long has it hurt?"

"It doesn't."

He leveled his gaze at her. "How long?"

"It's—"

"Not going to do us any good if you collapse. Altitude sickness is serious. Your brain swells. You can die. You can't just shrug it off."

She rubbed the space between her eyebrows again. "It's really not that bad."

"Dara," he warned.

She blew out a breath and met his eyes. "A few days."

A few days. He worked his jaw. So it had started even before she'd joined up with him. "And you didn't think you should mention it?"

"I didn't think…it would be a problem."

More likely, she'd been afraid he'd refuse to take her with him if he'd known.

He studied the determined glint in her eyes, the set to her jaw, and swore. She was the most stubborn woman he'd ever met.

But altitude sickness wasn't something to toy with. Taking a risk like this could get her killed.

And he'd made it worse. He'd forced her over higher terrain instead of sticking to the lower route, and all for nothing. That blasted sniper still dogged their steps.

He exhaled, searched for options, but there were none. He had to get her down the mountain fast. And then they needed to stay at a lower elevation for a day or two until she'd acclimated to the thinner air.

But if they stopped to rest, the sniper would catch them.

He swore again, unable to shake the nagging sense of danger. "We've still got a thousand feet to climb before we reach that pass," he told her. "I'm afraid your head's going to hurt worse before we can get you to lower ground."

"Don't worry." She scraped in another breath. "I'll be fine."

He hoped. In the meantime, he couldn't let her move around and waste her breath. "You'd better ride."

"But Rupper—"

"Is stronger than you are." He closed the distance between them and lifted her into the saddle, ignoring the pain that jolted his arm. "I'll lead him. All you have to do is hang on."

She swayed in the saddle, and his fear for her grew. As weak as she was, she'd be lucky not to plunge off the horse.

He pulled a small plastic bag from his shirt pocket and took out some leaves. "Have you chewed coca before?"

"No." She took the leaves from his hand.

"Ball them up and stick them in your cheek. Don't chew. Squeeze the leaves into a pulp, let the juice come out. It'll help your head." He hoped. The only real cure was to get her down to a safer altitude fast.

He watched her for a moment to make sure she put the leaves in her mouth, then started hiking again, leading the blowing, sweating horse. The only way he could stop the sniper now was to block the trail—if he could find a place to set the charge. He studied the boulders gleaming in the patchy moonlight, the dark crevices creasing the hills. Ruins dotted the slopes, ancient remnants of people long gone—the Inca, Wari…

An owl hooted in the pre-dawn air. The cool wind rustled the grass. Life was brief in these mountains, insignificant. Civilizations came and went like a puff of wind. And pleasure was even more fleeting.

He glanced at Dara as she clung to the horse, and his thoughts whipped back to that kiss. Maybe he was a fool to resist her. Maybe he should take what she offered and stop trying to do the right thing. She was an adult. She wanted him. And he sure as hell wanted her. Those ripe, sultry curves, that warm, velvet flesh made his blood run hot, his body pulse with heat.

But her hesitation had stopped him, the innocent way she watched him and blushed.

Innocent? He scoffed. Not likely. Not when she kissed like that. Plus, she'd admitted she didn't follow the rules.

So why didn't he do the same—forget the past, and do what nature intended? Life was short. And it had been too damned long since he'd lain in a woman's arms.

He slid his gaze to Dara again. She listed precariously in the saddle, hanging on by sheer determination, and a sudden warmth unfurled in his chest. And he knew the real reason he was reluctant to touch her. There was something different about this woman, something special. She was courageous, idealistic, dangerous.

She was the type of woman men fought for. The type who

stirred a man up for a noble cause, convinced him to march off to war. The type who tempted him to sacrifice everything for ideals, and believe in dreams.

But he'd stopped dreaming long ago.

He tightened his grip on the reins, led the horse around a boulder that jutted into the muddy trail. His wife's murder had shattered the last of his illusions, taught him the futility of hope. There was no point trying to slay the dragons in this world because justice didn't exist. Corruption and greed always won.

No matter what this woman believed.

Loose pebbles rolled under his boots, drawing his attention back to the trail. The path veered sharply ahead, narrowing to a small channel through the dirt and rocks. He stopped, sucked in the too-thin air, followed the trail of stones with his gaze. Even in the dim light he could see that the earth had sheered off and collapsed in a landslide, probably caused by an earthquake decades ago.

But if the earth had moved before, he could make it happen again.

He studied what he could of the narrow trail, then glanced at Dara again. She sat hunched over Rupper's neck, barely holding on, a picture of exhaustion and pain. He was doing a lousy job of keeping her safe so far.

"I want you to continue up the trail and wait for me at the top," he told her, surprised by the effort it took to talk. Even as acclimated to the mountains as he was, the lack of oxygen made it hard to speak. "I'm going to set a charge, bring down more rocks to block the trail."

She straightened. "You think…the sniper…"

"I don't know. But this should stop him if he's behind us. There's no other way up this slope." He'd have to hike around the peak, which would buy them some much-needed time. They could rest, let Dara recover in that cave for a day or two, without worrying about getting attacked.

"I'll help," she said, and struggled to dismount.

"The hell you will." Disgusted, he strode back to the horse and pushed her into the saddle again. "You're too weak to outrun a dynamite blast. Ride to the top of the hill and wait for me there."

"But—"

"For God's sake, Dara. Could you do what I ask for once? Running around will make the altitude sickness worse."

She opened her mouth as if to argue, then pressed her fingers to her forehead and winced. "All right."

Hoping she obeyed this time, he handed her the reins, pulled a flashlight, dynamite and fuse from the pack. Then he slapped Rupper's rump and sent him plodding up the slope.

Hurrying now, he picked his way across the unstable hill, slipping and sliding between the rocks. He flashed the light over the debris, spotted a crevice in a pile of boulders where he could set the charge.

It wouldn't be easy. He had to light the fuse, run back across the unstable slope, then sprint up the trail to the horse. And he wouldn't have much time before the dynamite blew.

He wished he knew what was above him. He flicked the light up the slope, but the beam didn't penetrate far. Still, he had to risk it. This was the only way to keep Dara safe.

His pulse beating hard now, he stuffed the dynamite into the crevice and lit the fuse. *Sixty seconds.* He trained his flashlight on the fuse, waited a second to make sure it took, then ran as fast as he could toward the trail. The pale beam bobbed over the uneven ground. The moist soil shifted under his feet. He slipped, slid downhill, nearly lost his balance and fell.

He righted himself, skidded again, and urgency surged through his nerves. Forty seconds. He had to get off this slope fast.

He dodged a boulder, continued racing toward the trail. Twenty seconds. But then he slid again, skidded several more meters downhill, and a harsh buzz rocked through his skull.

Damn. He was running out of time.

His vision blurred as he picked up speed. Adrenaline poured through his veins. He reached the trail, sprinted uphill, rasping and hauling in air. Ten seconds. Five.

Dread gripped his gut. A clammy sweat beaded his skin. He had to make it. He couldn't leave Dara—

The earth jolted, shifted, knocked him off his feet, and a huge blast boomed in his ears. He hit the ground, grabbed at a nearby tree, but his injured arm gave way. He rolled in a river of dirt and rocks down the slope, unable to stop, unable to breathe.

A rock glanced off his injured shoulder, and he groaned at the fierce stab of pain. He covered his head, slid down the mountain, buried in the earth and debris.

And thought of the woman he'd left behind.

Dara waited on the trail atop the restless horse, a whisper of unease brushing her nerves. The wind had died; the storm moved off behind the still-dark hills. Even the booms from the dynamite blast had faded into an eerie, throbbing silence.

There was no sign of life in the oppressive night, no sign of Logan. Only that unnerving, pulsing hush.

She shivered, wheezed in the cool air to steady her nerves. "Logan?" she called, shocked at the effort it took to speak. Her muscles felt weak. Dizziness twirled through her head. And a sharp ache pounded her forehead with an intensity that made her breath catch.

But she couldn't just sit here and gasp for air. Logan had told her to wait, but what if he was injured—or worse?

Dread coiled in her belly, seeped into her throat. "Logan," she called again, and her voice cracked.

Stark silence echoed back.

She rubbed her arms, glanced around at the ominous darkness, made out the silhouette of a tree up the trail. She urged the horse forward, tugged him to a stop when they were even with the tree.

Mercifully, the gelding was too tired to move as she struggled to dismount. Her movements were so slow, so clumsy that it took forever to reach the ground. Then she clung to the saddle to catch her breath.

But she couldn't afford to be weak. She straightened, forced herself to stagger toward the tree. She reached the small pine an eternity later, knotted the reins around a branch.

"I'll...be...back," she wheezed to Rupper, and he twitched his ears.

She paused for a moment to haul in air, then tied her knapsack to one of the packs. She hated to let it out of her sight, but she was too weak to haul it around. That done, she started down the trail. Her footsteps thudded on the muddy earth. The scent of fresh rain permeated the air. But there was no movement on the darkened hillside, no trace of life.

A sudden panic made her heart race, but she shoved the worry aside. Logan was all right. He had to be all right. He was too strong, too fearless to die.

She pictured his determined face, the lethal glint in his eyes. He was a survivor. His skill with his weapons, the sheer strength of his will made him a formidable man to defeat.

But he also had a haunting sense of loneliness about him. He worked alone, traveled in solitude on remote mountain peaks. And she had the impression that beyond that rugged shell lay a man with a wounded heart.

A man in pain.

She should know. All her life, she'd felt that same loneliness, that same desolation she sensed inside of him.

Maybe that was why she responded to him so strongly. She glanced around at the shrouded hillside. She was attracted to him physically, of course. She'd never met a sexier man. But she also felt a connection with him, a link that went beyond physical attraction, beyond what a duty-bound princess should feel for her mountain guide. There was something inevitable, something fated about Logan Burke.

Something that felt perfectly right.

She slipped on a patch of loose stones, forced her attention back to the trail. She would analyze her feelings for Logan later when they were safe. Right now she had to concentrate on finding the man—and pray that he wasn't hurt.

A boulder blocked the trail a few steps later, and she stopped. Silence drummed in the darkness. Dust from the dynamite blast lingered in the air.

Then a grunt came from farther down the slope, and her hopes surged. "Logan?"

"Over here."

He was alive. Relief barreled through her. She exhaled and closed her eyes.

But where was he? Why wasn't he on the trail? She jerked her eyes open again. "Where are you? Are you all right?"

"Yeah." He grunted again. "But my foot's caught under a rock."

She frowned into the shadowy darkness, unsure what to do. She'd never get the horse down there. The slope was too steep, the soil unstable. She'd have to free him alone.

"I'll be right there," she told him.

"No! Stay back," he said. "The rocks are about to come loose."

She ignored him, started picking her way through the dirt, but her steps sent stones tumbling, and she bit her lip. Logan was below her on the slope somewhere. The dislodged rocks could hit him, start a landslide, bury him in debris.

But it was hard to be careful when she could barely lift her feet. She plodded across the crumbling hill, moving as fast as she dared, panting and gasping for breath. Her head grew lighter with every step. Black spots clouded her eyes. She paused, braced her hands on her knees, struggled to haul in air.

She couldn't let herself faint, couldn't succumb to the exhaustion, or the terrible pain slamming her skull. Logan needed her help.

She forced herself to start walking again, ignored her leg muscles trembling with fatigue, the waves of dizziness pummeling her head. She finally spotted a pile of boulders in the dim light and stopped. "Logan?"

She scanned the rocks, spotted him lying to the side. "Logan?" she called again, but he didn't move, didn't respond.

Her stomach swooped. She rushed toward him, skidding in the loose stones and mud, saw where his foot angled under the rock. "Are you all right?"

He lifted his head then, and even in the poor light she could see his scowl. "What are you doing? I told you to stay off the hill. The whole damned thing's about to collapse."

And he'd go with it. She eyed the boulders, unsure what to do. They loomed over her in the dusky light, huge granite chunks, far too heavy to budge. But no matter how impossible it looked, she had to try. "I'll push."

"No! It's too risky. Get away."

"But—"

"Dara, get out of here. Just toss me a stick, something strong I can use as a lever to pry it off. Then get back on the trail."

She studied the pile of rocks, realized that he was right. One wrong move and those boulders would crush them both. So how could she dig him out? She gave a wistful thought to the small crowbar in her backpack. But she'd left it with the horse—too far away.

She peered around at the barren landscape, finally spotted a badly bent tree not far up the slope, its branches twisting through the rubble like broken spokes. "I'll be…right back."

Gasping, she worked her way to the tree. Her leg muscles shook. Her vision dimmed, and dark spots swelled in her eyes. But she found a stout, loose branch, somehow dragged it back to Logan and started working it under the rock.

"Give it to me," he said.

She ignored him, pushed on the branch as hard as she could, but the boulder didn't budge.

She needed to use more force. She rose on trembling legs, balanced over the branch. Her vision faded even more. Using every ounce of strength she had, she thrust herself down on the branch.

The boulder moved. Logan squirmed, yanked his foot loose. "Got it!"

Relief surged through her. She fell to her knees, blinded by the dark fog misting her eyes. The rocks made a sudden crack.

"Watch out!" Logan called, but his voice came from too far away.

The sound of grinding rocks split the air. The earth rumbled under her feet. She blinked, tried to crawl away from the boulders before they pulled her down, but the hillside shifted and slid.

She fell, reached blindly for Logan. And missed.

Chapter 9

"Dara!" Logan lunged for her as she collapsed on the shifting slope. He slammed to the ground, covered her with his bigger body to shelter her from the plunging rocks. Dirt rained on his back, his head. A boulder bounced past, clipping his calf, and he grunted at the fiery shock.

But he ignored the pain, jerked up his head to check for more falling rocks, then awkwardly surged to his feet. The earth was moving, roaring beneath his feet, the slope disintegrating in a sea of mud.

He swore. The entire mountain was coming apart. He had to get out of here fast.

He hefted Dara into his arms, dashed through the falling debris. Rocks collided and crashed around him. The mountain pitched and buckled below. But he charged through the sliding earth, dodged rocks that barreled out of the darkness, struggling against the current of mud.

He reached the trail, glanced around wildly, but the path to the top was now blocked. Sweat streamed down his jaw. His injured shoulder burned.

But he had to get up that slope. He turned, slogged straight up against the rushing mud, fighting for purchase on the treacherous earth. He blocked out the noise, the dust, just lowered his head and climbed, fueled by adrenaline, the frantic need to keep Dara alive.

The earth stopped moving an eternity later, and he paused. He coughed on dust, shifted Dara in his arms, turned and surveyed the disaster below.

Even in the dim light he could see the destruction. The dynamite had sheared off the side of the mountain, obliterated the trail, piling massive boulders along a broad swath. It would take the sniper at least a day to detour that mess.

Unless he knew these mountains better than Logan did.

He shoved that worry aside. Their pursuer couldn't be that good. The landslide had bought them some time—time he desperately needed, because Dara wasn't out of danger yet.

She curled towards him then, instinctively seeking comfort, and he switched his attention to her. His gaze roamed her face, her lips, her throat. Dirt smudged her cheeks. Her braid had come undone, and her dark hair clung to her skin like ribbons of ebony silk.

And he had the sudden urge to slide his mouth over hers, to taste her heat, her lips, and prove to himself she was safe.

Except she wasn't home free yet. He had to get her over the pass and down to a lower elevation before more fluid swelled in her brain.

Her eyes fluttered open, and she moaned. "Hang on, darlin'," he said, his fear for her making his voice rough.

"But…the sniper—"

"He's gone. Just rest."

He turned, continued hiking up the slope, his strained shoulder pulsing with every step. But he pushed aside the pain, focused on reaching his horse. He'd rest his arm once Dara was safe.

She stirred again when they reached his horse. He lifted her into the saddle, debated tying her in place. "Can you hold on?" he asked.

"Yes, I..." She wove, nearly fell. He leaped to catch her, but she pulled herself upright again. He shook his head, amazed by how determined she was, even in her weakened state.

How stubborn. She refused to follow instructions, recklessly put herself in danger, ignored her own safety to rescue him. She was driven, daring, infuriating.

Perfect.

The thought zapped through his mind like a bolt of rogue lightning, and he took a quick step back. Where had that come from? He couldn't like this woman. Not that way. He had to think of her as a job.

Lust was one thing. He'd have to be dead not to appreciate her sultry curves. But he didn't have relationships, didn't have a future—not with her, not anyone. Not anymore. He worked alone, lived alone. Life was simpler, and safer, that way.

He grabbed Rupper's reins, started hiking toward the pass, spooked by how tempting she was. And he knew that he had to be careful. This woman was different, dangerous. She was steadily eroding his defenses, cracking his rigid self-control.

But he'd already made too many mistakes, carried enough guilt to last this lifetime. He refused to add Dara to his list of regrets, no matter how appealing she was.

Unless she just wanted sex....

He groaned, jerked his mind away from that track. He'd vowed to keep her safe, and that's exactly what he'd do—even from himself.

Now he had to convince his body of that.

* * *

Fat chance, he decided several hours later.

They'd made it over the pass and down the mountain. Now he stood before her in the cavelike entrance to the mine shaft, his hands gripping her shirt. She was exhausted, incoherent, so cold she couldn't speak. She'd been trying to undress, to remove her wet clothes, but her hands were too icy and stiff.

And now it was up to him to strip off her clothes and bundle her in those blankets before she froze.

Right. His fingers literally trembled. He gritted his teeth, concentrated on working the buttons through the holes, ignoring how his knuckles grazed her full breasts. He could do this, he told himself grimly. He could stay in control, stay detached, keep his mind off his sexual needs.

He peeled off her wet shirt, and his gaze whipped to her breasts like a heat-seeking missile, completely beyond his control.

They were perfect—ripe, lush curves encased in a provocative scrap of sheer lace. Full and high, with dark, taut nipples begging for his hands, his tongue.

His breath turned shallow and fast. His body tightened with need. He reached for the back clasp on her bra, unhooked it, and the scrap of lace peeled away.

He closed his eyes, inhaled, battled to block out the sight, but the image of those dark, tempting nipples was seared in his brain. He couldn't breathe, didn't dare move. He was rooted in place, the need for her knotting his veins.

But she stepped back, hugged herself, her teeth chattering. And he jerked his mind from the lust.

"Stand still," he rasped, his voice hoarse. He reached for her jeans, fumbled with the button, felt the cool, smooth silk of her skin. The need to yank her against him, immerse his hard, heavy length in her heat nearly did him in.

But he lowered himself to one knee, peeled down her pants. Sweat beaded his brow. He turned his head, tried not to look at the dark, lush triangle beckoning between her thighs, or inhale her erotic scent.

She braced her cold hand on his shoulder for balance, and he tugged the wet denim off. Her braid had come undone, and as she bent to help him, her damp silky hair slid past his jaw.

He tossed her jeans aside, and rose. "Get under the covers," he ground out.

She slid under the alpaca blankets, and he turned, sucked in the cave's musty air, trying to clear his mind of her scent. But it didn't work. Every soft, velvet inch of her had been branded in his mind.

He knew he was far too close to the edge, veering toward losing control. He needed to walk away, cool off before he did something he would regret. But she was shaking, shuddering so loudly he could hear her from where he stood. And he couldn't let her freeze.

Swearing, knowing he was a fool for tempting fate, he jerked off his own clothes, slipped under the blankets with her. He pulled her against him, tugged her smooth, creamy body to his, surrounding her with his heat.

She fit him perfectly. Her smooth back molded his chest. Her soft, rounded bottom curved into his groin. He splayed his hand on her hip, flexed his fingers, fought to keep from stroking her breasts, her thighs.

She put her feet on his shins, and the icy shock made him groan. All she wanted was warmth. And he was so aroused he couldn't breathe.

Several endless minutes later, her shivering eased. Her breath steadied, grew deeper, and he knew that she was asleep. He rolled over, turning his back to her, staying close enough so she could feel his heat. It didn't help.

And he forced himself to face the hard truth. He didn't have the self-control he'd believed he had around this woman. He wanted her. She'd become a need in his blood, a craving he couldn't contain.

Hunger whipped through his nerves, the scent of her pulsed through his brain. And he knew it was no use. He had to have her.

Soon.

She'd said she didn't follow the rules. So maybe she'd be willing to just have sex.

As soon as she gave him a signal, he would find out.

Dara awoke late that afternoon in a makeshift bed. She snuggled into the soft alpaca blankets on the packed earth floor, sighed at the lingering comfort of Logan's scent. Memories flickered back, images of plodding down the mountain on the horse, Logan removing her rain-soaked clothes.

The searing heat of his skin as he held her close.

She jerked her eyes open. Oh, God. He'd been in bed with her. Naked.

She sat up, clutched the blankets to her bare chest, quickly scanned the dim cave. She spotted him crouched by a campfire outside the entrance. His worn jeans molded his muscled thighs, his shirt hugged his sculpted back. He'd left his hat by the packs, and his black hair gleamed in the flickering light.

He turned his head, as if sensing her watching, and his dark gaze drove into hers. And his sexual appeal slammed through her again, at how thoroughly male he looked with that desperado beard stubble darkening his jaw, the enthralling strength of his arms.

His gaze narrowed, heated, then inched deliberately over her, and her face turned hot. She knew she looked a mess, her long hair all tumbled over her bare shoulders. She tugged the blanket to her chin, smoothed back her hair, unsure whether to be embarrassed or grateful that he'd removed her wet clothes.

Because he'd certainly seen plenty of skin.

And from the rapt, predatory way he watched her, she knew he remembered that, too.

"How's your head?" he asked, his voice deep.

"Better." Her forehead still pounded, but the pain was fainter now, more bearable. "It doesn't ache as much."

"Good." His dark gaze roved over her again, lingering on her lips, her breasts, and her heart made a frenzied lurch.

"I'm going to check on Rupper," he said. He motioned toward the campfire. "There's tea here, *mate de coca*. It'll help with the headache. The stew still needs to heat for a while." He rose in a strong, fluid motion that made her breath catch, turned on his heel, and strode off.

She hitched in a breath, waited to make sure he'd really left, then dressed in the spare clothes from her pack. By the time she'd wandered over to the campfire Logan had built, her breathing had nearly returned to normal.

Now if only she could steady her pulse. She took the coffee pot from the fire, poured the steaming tea into the tin cup he'd set aside, then perched on a nearby rock. And she knew the time had come to make a decision. This attraction between them, this searing, blinding need, was driving her out of her mind. Every time she looked at the man, she ached to throw herself into his arms.

But did she dare do it? Could she ignore a lifetime of rules, break her people's strictest taboo?

She was their princess, their leader—soon to be the queen, once the mourning for her parents had passed. And she had to be an example, had to behave better than most. And that meant obeying the rules, including remaining a virgin until she wed.

But who would ever know? She'd decided long ago she'd never marry unless she fell in love. And since that had never happened—and wasn't likely to at her age—why shouldn't she lie with Logan? Why shouldn't she experience bliss with this virile man? He was everything she'd ever dreamed of, the most thrilling man she'd ever met.

And could she really bear to go back home, to return to a lifetime of loneliness, without ever knowing his touch?

Footsteps thudded beyond the cave, interrupting her thoughts, and then Logan appeared on the path. He slowed, and his dark gaze arrowed on hers. Her heart lost its rhythm. Her breath turned erratic again.

"Thanks for the tea and…everything," she said, sounding breathless.

"No problem." His gaze dipped to her mouth, and her heart went crazy again.

She cleared her throat, shocked by how badly she ached to step close to him, to run her fingers along his jaw, to feel his big calloused hands stroking her skin. "What happened to the sniper?"

He tossed her a bag of beef jerky, then settled on the rock across from her, braced his forearms on his knees. "The landslide blocked the trail. It will take him a day or two to get around. We can rest until morning, give you time to recover before we go on."

She swallowed a bite of jerky, tore her gaze from his beautifully sculpted arms. Despite his assurances, there was an underlying tension in his voice. She sensed they didn't have much time to spare. "We can leave now. I don't need to rest."

"Sure you do." His dark brows gathered in a frown. "Your body needs to adjust to the lower oxygen level up here."

"But I really don't feel bad. Not anymore. My headache's almost gone and I'm not so out of breath."

"You'll relapse if we climb too soon."

"It's not too soon. I'm okay, really. I—"

"Forget it, Dara." He scowled at her. "Why the hell do you have to argue about everything? The air's thin this high up, and your body needs time to adapt. It happens to everyone. It doesn't mean you're weak."

"I…" She closed her mouth. He was right. She despised being weak, hated to ask for help. Her people depended on her to be strong. Her parents had drilled that into her since birth.

"A lot of people have bigger problems than I do," she finally said. "It seems…self-indulgent to worry about myself when I'm really not bad off."

"Altitude sickness can kill you," he said. "It's not something you can ignore. And if you're used to living at sea level, it takes time to adjust to the thinner air."

She considered that as she sipped her coca tea. She'd been born in Romanistan, lived there as a toddler, and it was as mountainous as Peru. But then civil war erupted and her family had been exiled. "I guess that's true. My parents were professors, so we lived in different university towns, but never anywhere high."

"They were archeologists, too?"

"No, they taught political science and history." Roma history. And they'd expected her to do the same. "Archeology was my dream." The one indulgence she'd fought for. Fortunately, pursuing the fabled Roma dagger had given her an excuse to do what she loved—at least for now.

The corner of Logan's mouth ticked up, sending sensual flutters through her nerves. "You wanted to be Indiana Jones?"

She smiled. "More like Hiram Bingham. I've always wanted to explore Peru, to discover lost Inca cities." She'd dreamed of it, spent her life yearning for freedom, adventure.

And Peru was an archeologist's fantasy, from the Moche

pyramids and Nazca lines, to the Incan mummies interred on mountain peaks.

But this was the closest she would ever come to living that fantasy. Once she found that dagger, she had to go back home and assume her royal role.

She sipped the tea, watched the afternoon storm clouds gather over the slopes. Distant thunder rumbled, drumming the earth beneath her feet, and the cool breeze fluttered her hair.

"It's so beautiful out here, so wild. It's exactly how I thought it would be." She eyed the steep slopes, the sheer granite slabs cloaked in the drifting mist. The land was ancient, mesmerizing. Almost as intriguing as Logan himself. "I wish I could stay here forever," she added.

"No, you don't. There's nothing here for a woman like you."

She blinked, turned to face him again, surprised at the certainty in his voice. "How can you say that? You don't know anything about me."

He raised his brows. "You could live in a mud hut without water and electricity?"

She pursed her lips, thought about how heavenly a long, steamy shower would feel right now. "Maybe not forever," she admitted. "But I wouldn't mind a compromise, spending a few months of the year out here."

The thought took hold as she sipped her tea. And she realized that if she didn't have obligations, if she weren't a royal princess, she would want this life, this man.

He bent to stir the stew simmering over the fire, and the sheer masculine beauty of him made her breath catch. She studied the flat, male planes of his face, mesmerized by the way the firelight glinted in his inky hair, the way his powerful shoulders flexed and rippled beneath his shirt.

He glanced up, and their gazes caught. His eyes narrowed,

darkened with a predatory intent, trapping her in his heat. Her hands began to shake, sending tea slopping over her cup.

She yanked her gaze to the hills, struggled to calm her racing nerves, knowing she was flirting with danger here. Having sex with Logan would be one thing. But she didn't dare dream of a life without duty. She had obligations, duties, responsibilities to her people.

And she accepted that. Maybe it wasn't her dream to be the queen, maybe she longed to have a more adventurous life, but she cared about the Roma. She didn't want her people to suffer. And it was her job to keep them safe.

But if she had a choice…

She sighed, knowing the futility of that thought. She shook herself back to reality, forced herself to meet Logan's gaze. "You're lucky you can live in the mountains. Not everyone can do what they want."

He scoffed. "I don't have much choice. There's nothing else I can do. My wife learned that fast enough."

Her heart stumbled hard. She gaped at him, so shocked she couldn't breathe. "You're married?"

"No." He scowled, drew back, looking as appalled as she was. "I'd never…she's dead."

"Oh." She yanked her gaze to her cup. Of course he'd have a romantic past. She shouldn't have been surprised. After all, he was a wildly attractive man.

And his wife's death explained his somber air. "I'm sorry," she added.

He rose, prowled to the edge of the path, then stood staring out toward the mountains, his hands planted low on his hips. She took in the unyielding set to his jaw, the tension in his wide back, and he looked so isolated suddenly, so utterly lonely, that a deep ache formed in her chest.

Logan was lethal, powerful, dangerous. But beyond that

rugged shell was a complex man. A man who'd lost his wife, suffered tragedies, grieved. A man who needed human comfort and warmth.

And she knew with a sudden clarity that she was the woman to provide it.

Chapter 10

For a moment, Dara simply stood beside him. She watched the gathering storm steal over the land, the eucalyptus trees rustle and dip, felt the thunder vibrate the earth.

But as menacing as the oncoming storm was, she sensed the real torment was inside this man.

"What was your wife like?" she finally asked.

She thought at first he wouldn't answer, that maybe she'd crossed some forbidden line. But then he glanced at her, his eyes unreadable, and shrugged. "Beautiful, delicate. Pampered, but I didn't know that then."

"Was she Roma?"

"Yeah." He frowned at the mountains again. "My mother arranged the match. She thought if I married into a clan they'd take her back. And after she died…" He shook his head. "I'd given my word. It didn't seem right to back out."

Of course he would honor the agreement. She couldn't imagine him reneging on his word. "So what happened?"

"It was a bad match. We had nothing in common. María hated the mountains. She missed her family, wanted to live in Lima where she'd grown up."

"And you didn't want to live there?"

"I tried. We spent a year there, living in the slums. It was as bad as any gold mining town I'd seen. Poverty, disease. And I couldn't get a decent job. I never finished high school. Tracking and hauling freight is the only thing I can do."

She doubted that. As determined and intelligent as Logan was, he could do whatever he set his mind to. But she understood. These mountains suited him. She couldn't imagine him anywhere else. "So what happened?"

"I convinced her to come back here. I promised we'd move back to Lima when we had enough cash. But she was miserable. We fought all the time. She wouldn't come with me on my freight runs, then resented the time I spent away."

"She was young?" Dara guessed.

"Seventeen. But it wasn't just her age. We were too different. And she kept trying to get me to change."

Dara knew how that felt. Her parents had never understood her desire for adventure, had spent her entire childhood trying to make her conform.

"That last trip, I convinced her to come with me," Logan said. "But we got into one of our usual fights. She threatened to go back to Lima, get a divorce, and then she rode off. I let her go. I thought she'd cool down and come back. When she didn't, I went to find her. But by the time I did…"

His jaw tightened. And the sudden, haunting bleakness in his eyes chilled her heart. "She'd been raped and murdered on her way into town."

Shock jolted through her. She pressed her hand to her throat.

"Oh, Logan. I'm so sorry." She drew in a breath, and the horror of what he must have seen swept through her. He'd found his dead wife, seen her violated, brutalized body.

She could only imagine the horrendous guilt he would feel. "You can't blame yourself," she said firmly. "You couldn't have known."

He made a sound of disgust. "I was her husband. I shouldn't have let her go."

"But—"

"I'd vowed to protect her. I'd given my word." His voice turned hard, and a muscle ticked in his cheek. "Hell, I didn't do anything right. I couldn't even find out who killed her. Whoever murdered her is still out there."

"You tried to find the killer?"

"For all the good it did." He worked his jaw. "The police didn't care. One less Gypsy didn't matter to them. I spent two years scouring the mountains, chasing dead ends. I hired detectives, paid bribes, spent every damned *sol* I had. But there were no clues, no witnesses. No one saw anything, or they were too afraid to say."

His voice vibrated with bitterness, pain, and her heart ached for this wounded man. He was a hard man, an honorable one. A man who wouldn't forgive his mistakes.

The wind gusted up the path, making the campfire leap, and she rubbed her arms against the chill. "Coping with death is hard," she said softly. "And murder..." She shivered, hugged herself. "My parents were shot. I was with them when it happened, and I still feel guilty that I survived.

"It wasn't my fault," she continued when his eyes met hers. "I know that. But it doesn't help. I keep wondering why they died, why I survived. I keep reliving that night over and over, thinking if I'd stood in a different spot, if I'd been paying more attention, that maybe..."

She shook her head, willing away the terror of that night, the violent memories that hadn't eased. "I've spent hours torturing myself, wondering *why* it happened. Was it fate? Or some random, senseless act?

"But there's no answer, no way to know. Nothing helps it make sense. It just happened. I think...some things just have to be accepted. They can't be rationalized or explained."

Like why fate had led her to this place, this man.

And why he felt so right.

His eyes held hers. And an understanding flickered between them, a feeling of empathy, comfort, warmth.

He stepped close, ran his thumb across her cheek. And a sudden desire surged through her, the need to hold him, caress him, to prove to him that she cared.

And that he was far more worthy than he thought.

"We just have to keep living," she said quietly. "That's all we can do. Live, and find pleasure in the time we have now."

His eyes darkened, stayed on hers, and her heart stumbled into her throat. He leaned closer, so close she inhaled the heat of his skin, felt his restless male energy throb in the air.

And solace turned to something deeper, something far more earthy. The raw, pulsing beat of desire.

"I'm all for pleasure," he rasped, and her lungs went still. "But that's all I can give you. Just pleasure, nothing more. I live alone, work alone. And that's not going to change. Not even for you."

"I would never want you to change." She reached up, traced the bullet graze on his cheek, the planes of his unshaven jaw, felt the rising heat sizzle her blood.

But he grabbed her wrist and stopped her. "Be damned sure, because I'm not playing games."

The husky growl of his deep voice thrilled her. Shivers of hunger streaked through her nerves. But beyond the desire, the pounding excitement, a deep certainty settled inside her, the knowledge that this was right.

The rules she'd grown up with didn't apply here. This was the right man, the right time, the right place. He needed her. And she desperately wanted him.

"I'm sure," she whispered and stepped close.

His gaze turned hotter, stayed deliberately locked on hers. Her knees grew weak. Her breath turned shallow and fast.

He kept one hand clamped on her wrist, used the other to unbutton her shirt. The sides parted. He unhitched her bra, his eyes still hot on hers, and the cool breeze brushed her bare skin.

She knew he was testing her, challenging her, giving her one last chance to back out.

She didn't move.

And then his gaze dipped, making a long, slow slide over her breasts.

Her breath locked up. Her heart stumbled in her chest. And pleasure shocked through her, making her lips part, her knees sag, her bare breasts tighten and swell. And all he'd done was look at her. She trembled and closed her eyes.

"You're so damned beautiful," he ground out. "You make me burn." He shifted closer and gently, almost reverently, cupped one breast with his callused hand. She shuddered at the delirious contact, struggled to drag in air. He leaned into her, enveloping her in his heat, his strength, pulling her hips to his, making her vibrantly aware of his need.

And then his mouth claimed hers in a hot, drugging kiss that scalded every nerve. He made a low, raw sound and hauled her against him, and the incredible, sensual feel of him, all hard angles and bulging strength, sent a torrent of desire through her blood.

She sagged against him, lost in his kiss, his touch, so over-whelmed by the delirious feel of him that all she could do was moan. She was beyond thought, beyond control, totally at the mercy of this man. And she didn't care. No matter what happened later, she knew this could never be wrong.

Wanting to memorize him, to feel every masculine inch of him, she slid her hands up his arms. She twined her hands in his hair, stroked his taut, sinewed neck, felt the thrill of his rough, bristled jaw.

His kiss deepened, growing bolder, more relentless. His big hands roved down her back, flexed on her hips, and then he cupped her bottom, lifted her slightly, pressing her tightly against his arousal. Her nerves jolted and skipped, like fireworks bursting in her veins.

He tore his mouth from hers, and she gasped. "Don't stop."

"Not a chance." His smile was lethal, wicked, his voice an erotic growl. The world twirled as he lifted her into his arms, carried her into the cave to the blankets spread over the ground.

"Your shoulder—"

"Forget it." He laid her down gently, leaned over her, bracing his weight on his uninjured arm. His dark eyes continued to caress her, his blatant hunger ignited her blood.

And the sight of him, the planes of his face drawn taut, his eyes nearly black with desire, made everything feminine inside of her go soft.

He tugged off her shirt. And then he lowered his hands and mouth to her breasts, and the shock of it, the hot, carnal feel of it, caused pleasure so raw that she moaned.

She spiked her hands in his hair, felt his hard shoulders tighten and flex. And she surged against him, lost to the feel of his mouth on her skin, the electric heat of his tongue.

And then he kissed her again, their tongues mating in a wild, scorching duel that set off a frenzy of need. She thrilled to his hands, his skin, his mouth. She twisted against him, wanting to feel him everywhere, with an urgency she couldn't control.

He paused, jerked off his shirt. And she stroked her hands down his chest, felt the hard muscles ripple and bunch. And then he unsnapped her jeans, slid his hand down her belly, and suddenly, she couldn't breathe.

She closed her eyes, ravaged by the deep, pulsing ache surging through her. "Logan," she moaned. She'd never felt pleasure so torrid. And she knew she'd die if he stopped.

His mouth claimed hers, his tongue mimicking the motion of his hand, causing an ache too exquisite to bear. And all she could do was surrender to the hunger, the urgency rocking her blood. The need grew frantic, insistent, and she pressed against him with a wildness she couldn't contain.

His dark, sensual laugh ripped through her nerves. "Steady, darlin'. We've got all night."

"But…" His fingers slid inside her, magical, slick, and a long moan escaped her lips. And she couldn't move, couldn't think, the need so raw she wanted to scream.

But then he stopped.

She opened her eyes, dazed by the ache pulsing through her, the frantic urgency hammering her veins. "What—?"

"You're a virgin." His eyes burned black, the planes of his face drawn stark. "You're a bloody virgin."

She could hardly deny it. "It doesn't matter." She clutched his shoulders, bucked against him, struggled to pull him close.

It was like trying to budge all of Peru.

"Like hell it doesn't matter." He jerked out of her grasp and sat up. "How old are you, anyway?"

She blinked, confused, her mind still rocked by desire. "Twenty-seven, but—"

"And you've never married?" He sounded so appalled that her face grew hot.

"No, and I don't intend to." She buttoned her jeans, tugged on her shirt, embarrassment and frustration making her hands shake.

"Why not?"

Because she couldn't have him.

The thought spun through her, catching her off guard, but she instantly knew it was true. She did want him. Only him. But she couldn't tell him that. They'd only met a few days ago. He'd think she'd lost her mind.

Miserable, angry now, she rose, then stalked to the edge of the cave. She wanted to hit something, kick something. She felt so frustrated she wanted to cry.

"Why aren't you going to marry?" he demanded from behind her.

She wheeled back, goaded by his angry tone. He didn't want a future with her. He'd said so. So why did he even care?

"Because I don't want to," she snapped. "You said you had a lousy marriage. Well, I don't want an arranged marriage, either. I'll do everything else I have to. I'll find the dagger. I'll go back and lead my people. But I won't marry for some political reason. And I won't marry a man I don't love."

He stared down at her, his dark brows furrowed, his big hands braced on his hips. His eyes simmered with anger, intelligence. And she bit her lip, realizing exactly how much she'd let slip.

And then he stilled, and his expression turned even more dangerous. His voice dropped to a lethal growl. "I think, darlin', it's time you told me who you really are."

Misery chugged through her. A thick knot swelled in her throat. The charade was up. He'd just figured out who she was.

And any hopes that he'd touch her again, that he'd make wild and glorious love to her, died. "I told you. Dara... Adara—"

"Adamovich. Not Adams," he said, and anger vibrated his voice. He was thoroughly, coldly enraged. "Hell. You're the Roma princess."

Chapter 11

He'd almost dishonored the Roma princess.

Reeling, feeling as if an earthquake had jolted him off his feet, Logan stared at the woman before him. He'd seen a picture of her once, but he still hadn't made the connection. And suddenly it all made sense—her defiance, her unwillingness to follow orders, the fire in her exotic eyes.

He shoved his hand through his hair, then gripped the back of his neck, still trying to process it all. This daring, mule-headed, *reckless* woman was the princess. The sole surviving member of the royal family. And he'd nearly made love to her, nearly taken her virginity! Fate had to be mocking him, laughing hysterically at his plight.

Hell of a joke.

He hissed out a breath, locked his gaze on hers. She had her arms crossed, her chin raised in that familiar, stubborn tilt. She looked annoyed, grumpy. Frustrated. And he knew exactly what she wanted, what her body desired. He slid his gaze down her full, pouting breasts, over her sweetly curving hips. She was aroused, burning for him.

He closed his eyes, stifled a groan, the memory of her scorched into his brain. Her erotic scent. That luscious mouth. The sweet heaven of her moist, swollen flesh. He was still hard, still throbbing for her, ready to explode. And he knew even now he could go to her, give them both the relief they craved.

The hell he could. If she'd been off-limits before, this revelation created a chasm he could never breach. The woman was totally out of his league, completely forbidden to him, in too many ways to count.

He swore, opened his eyes, frustration turning his voice harsh. "How can you even be here? How can you be traipsing through the mountains alone?" The idea staggered him, completely boggled his mind. "Why isn't anyone protecting you?"

She whirled toward the entrance to the cave, putting her back to him, and that ticked him off even more. Princess or not, she wasn't going to evade his questions.

He stalked around her, putting himself directly in her line of vision, forcing her to look up and meet his eyes. "Where are your bodyguards?" he demanded.

Her full lips turned down in a mutinous expression, and she scowled. "They don't know where I am. No one does."

He stared at her, unable to believe he'd heard right. "You snuck off on your own?" Could this situation get any worse?

"I didn't have a choice." She huffed out her breath in a sigh. "Look, I told you my parents were murdered."

He remembered the story. It had even made headlines here, in this remote part of the world. The ancient Roma necklace had been discovered in a Spanish bank vault, part of a cache of forgotten Nazi war loot. Hoping to downplay the scandal and appease the Gypsies, Spain decided to donate the necklace to them. But just as the exiled king and queen were about to accept the necklace, they'd been shot.

The story had all the elements of a tabloid thriller—an ancient legend, a curse, even a deranged secret society bent on destroying the Roma worldwide. The media had gone berserk.

He gazed down at Dara's determined face, and his sympathy stirred. It must have been hell for her to see her parents killed.

"The police thought the Black Crescent society would come after me, too," she continued, referring to the group that had murdered her parents. "So I went into hiding, into protective custody in California. That's where I've been until now."

"You should have stayed there."

"I couldn't." Her eyes met his. "I told you a man broke into my apartment a few weeks ago and tried to find my notes about the dagger. He also murdered one of my guards."

A haunted look slid into her eyes, and she hugged her arms. "I couldn't put anyone else in danger. Too many innocent people have already died. And I couldn't bear to be responsible for another death. So I left."

And put herself in danger instead. His outrage grew. "And no one stopped you? They just let you go?" What kind of idiotic guards did she have?

"I wasn't under arrest." Her dark eyes flashed. "And no one *lets* me do anything. I don't have a boss."

"Well, you should." He scowled down at her. "Coming here was reckless. Dangerous."

Her chin came up, and she shook her head, sending her loose hair shimmering down her back. "I thought I'd be safe. No one knows where I went. The police aren't going to announce that I've left. And out here I'm just another archeologist, a tourist. No one pays any attention to me. The only people who know the truth are you and my academic advisor. He's the one who told me to contact you."

Stunned at the risk she'd taken, furious at the danger she'd put herself in, he leaned close and gripped her chin. The soft, fragile feel of her made him angrier yet. "You're wrong. That sniper knows where you are."

She bit her lip, and fear moved into her eyes. His temper turned darker yet.

He hissed, dropped his hand, then stalked to the edge of the cave. Rain inched over the mountains. Thunder cracked, then rattled the ground. The wind sprang up as the storm approached, raising goose bumps on his neck.

The danger was worse than he'd thought. That sniper wasn't only after treasure. He wanted to murder the princess, the last of the royal Roma line.

And it was up to Logan to stop him.

He tilted back his head, closed his eyes at the terrible irony. The sheer impossibility made him want to laugh. The royal line was in his hands. *His hands.* A man who'd failed to protect anyone who'd ever depended on him.

Hell, it was worse than that. He'd heard the rumors about that Black Crescent society—vicious, hate-filled nuts who were trying to eliminate the Roma, conquer Romanistan, and rule the world. An insane goal, but the struggle could lead to war, nuclear war in that volatile region, and wipe out half the globe.

He let out a low, bitter laugh. "You picked the wrong damned guide, darlin'."

"I don't think so."

"Haven't you been listening?" He wheeled around to face her, fury making his gut clench. "I can't protect you. I can't protect anyone. I'm the last man you should be with."

Her eyes held his. "You've done a good job so far."

"The hell I have." He'd dragged her over the mountain, almost lost her in a landslide, dropped her off a cliff. And then he'd nearly taken her virginity, nearly dishonored her—on the floor of a musty cave.

Appalled at himself, he strode over to his AK-47 and picked it up, then stuffed supplies in his pack.

"Where are you going?" Her voice turned high. "You're not leaving me?"

As if he would. He made a sound of disgust. He had no choice but to protect this woman, no matter what the cost.

He'd probably die trying.

So be it. He hefted his pack, and a deep sense of resignation slid through his gut. He glanced at her, saw the anxiety lurking in her eyes, and he forced himself to gentle his words. She had enough to face in the days ahead without his bad temper worrying her more. "Eat some stew. Get some sleep. We'll head out at dawn."

"But…where are you going?"

"To check on Rupper." Patrol, clean his weapons, stand guard.

And sleep outside where he wouldn't be tempted to touch her again.

"But I thought…the sniper…you said he couldn't—"

"I don't know what he'll do." And he couldn't take any chances, not with the princess' life at stake. He needed to think this out, anticipate the sniper's moves, not give him a chance to catch up. He strode toward the entrance to the cave.

"Logan."

He paused, turned to face her again. Her face was still flushed, her lips swollen from his kiss. Her long black hair tumbled down her back. Even in jeans, she looked regal, every inch the princess. And too damned desirable.

"You're wrong," she whispered. "You're the strongest, most

heroic man I've ever met. I wouldn't want to be here with anyone else."

He shook his head, and a bleak feeling seeped through his gut. He wished it were true, wished he could be the man she believed, that he could escape the damning past. But he couldn't change who he was.

"I'm not the man you think. And wishing won't change that fact." The edge of his mouth slid back. "They lied to you, Dara. Fairy tales don't come true, not even for a princess like you."

The problem with not sleeping, Dara decided as she listened to the rain drumming off the rocks outside the cave in the pre-dawn darkness, wasn't the exhaustion. It wasn't the aching head, the cranky temper, the gritty eyes or fatigue. It was that she had too many hours to think.

She groaned, twisted in the blankets, tried to get comfortable on the rocky earth. She'd spent the first half of the night too aroused to sleep. Hour after hour she'd kept reliving those delirious sensations—Logan's kiss, the ecstasy of his hands on her skin, the thrill of his huge, hard body on hers. Her breasts ached. Tremors of desire rippled through her. Desire surged and throbbed through her veins.

He'd left her burning, suffering, remembering every single detail of how he'd felt, how he'd moved. And she'd wanted desperately to go to him, to demand that he free her from the unending hunger, that he finish what they'd begun.

Pride had kept her in the cave. Pride and guilt.

Because eventually, the long hours and hard floor had taken their toll, letting the urgency fade, letting the need for Logan subside to a simmering ache. And then her thoughts had turned inward.

She hadn't liked what she'd found.

She rolled over again, jerked the blankets to her chin with

a sigh. She felt guilty, all right. She knew she had a tendency to ride roughshod over people. It was a legacy from her parents, two crusaders completely immersed in their cause. They had stampeded through their lives, ignoring anyone and anything not related to their political agenda—just stubbornly forging on.

And she'd done the same thing to Logan. She'd pulled him into her fight, endangered his life, forced him to relive his painful past.

All for a cause he didn't believe in.

She stared into the darkness, shivered as the damp wind moaned through the cave, and tried to sort through her tangled thoughts. She had to find the dagger. She had no doubts about that. Her people needed it to survive.

But did she have a right to cause Logan harm in the process? Did she have a right to cause him pain for her people's sake?

And what could she do about it now?

She remembered the bleak look in his eyes as he spoke of his mother, his wife, and a thick feeling weighted her chest. He was a hard man with a wounded soul. A man punishing himself for events that weren't his fault.

A man she was dangerously close to falling in love with.

She pressed her hand to her lips at the thought. Was that true? Was she falling in love with Logan Burke? But how could she be? She'd only known him a couple of days.

But she knew the essentials. She knew he was an honorable, selfless man. An intensely idealistic man who'd been badly disillusioned, a warrior who cloaked his true nature with a cynical smile.

A man who didn't think he was a hero. But he'd plucked her from that cliff, rescued her from the sniper and thugs. He spent his life protecting the vulnerable miners—yet pretended he didn't care.

But he did care, deeply. He would never admit it, though. He was determined to live in exile, remain alone.

Could she change that? Could she prove he was the man she believed?

She frowned, turned that over in her mind. She'd always believed in fate, *kintala*. So maybe they were destined to come together. Maybe this man needed her as much as her people did. Maybe that was why she was here—to break through that cynicism and heal his damaged soul.

And maybe the lack of sleep had scrambled her brain.

She groaned, flipped to her other side, wriggled as the sharp rocks dug into her hip. She was probably crazy to think that fate had brought her to this man, and that she could heal his pain.

Especially since he'd warned her he wouldn't change.

But crazy or not, they were stuck in this ordeal together. And before it was over, she was going to try.

But by late the next afternoon, she had no idea how she could get through to him. Logan had completely withdrawn since he'd nearly made love to her in the cave.

They'd set off at a relentless pace at dawn, then spent the entire day riding in silence. They'd zigzagged over mountains, crossed hidden valleys, plodded through icy streams. The rain had subsided around noon, giving way to a chilly drizzle that kept her hunched against his broad back.

And he'd rebuffed her attempts at conversation, hardly spoken to her all day, except for an occasional curt question to make sure her headache hadn't returned. He rode with his jaw clenched, his eyes riveted on their surroundings, so on edge that tension vibrated off him in waves. Even during their rare breaks, he'd stalked away from her, as if he couldn't even stand to stay close.

But while he had ignored her, she had ping-ponged between

her mounting dread about the sniper, and being far too conscious of every movement Logan made—the brush of his back against her chest, the way his muscled thighs gripped the horse, the ease of his hands on the reins. She'd spent hours admiring the tendons in his corded forearms, the black stubble coating his jaw, the powerful width of his shoulders and back.

Reliving his kiss, his touch, his scent.

And by the time he signaled the horse to a halt at the entrance to a narrow valley, she was so wound up she wanted to shriek. "We'll rest here for a minute," he announced.

"Fine." Grateful for the reprieve, she slid off the horse, anxious to take her mind off Logan and settle her nerves. Something had to give soon. She couldn't take much more of his unnerving silence.

But one glance up the valley reminded her of the sniper, and that set her even more on edge. The valley itself looked benign enough—it was a steep, parched swath of land with a couple of brown mud huts clinging to one slope. But over the valley loomed a row of bloodred rocks arranged in oddly shaped formations. They looked ominous, menacing, like eerie sentinels standing watch.

Warning anyone who planned to venture into the canyon to leave.

Logan leaped down from the horse, looped the reins around a bush, then drew his rifle from the pack. So he felt the foreboding, too.

"Drink some water," he said, keeping his voice low. "I'm going to scout around."

She glanced at the deserted valley, and a strong sense of unease slithered through her. "You think the sniper could be nearby?"

"I doubt it. We had a good lead on him after that rockslide."

But something was wrong. His eyes were too grim, his

mouth even more somber than before. He strode off, disappeared from sight, and her nerves wrenched tighter yet. She sought the privacy of a bush, drank water from the canteen, more relieved than she cared to admit when he finally came back.

"Where are we?" she asked as he approached.

He slid his rifle into its holder, took the canteen. He drank deeply, his Adam's Apple dipping in his whiskered throat, then wiped his mouth on the back of his hand. "Quillacocha's on top of that peak." He nodded toward the mountain that crouched over the valley like a puma ready to strike. "There's a pilgrim's trail through here. The main Inca road comes in on the other side."

They were that close? She glanced at the colored rocks, the strange formations lining the cliffs, and her heart made a sudden skip. "This must be Yawar Rumi, the sacred valley." Named for the bloodred rocks. It was on a *ceque,* one of the imaginary lines that led from the Temple of the Sun in Cusco to holy sites throughout the Incan empire.

But that didn't explain Logan's tension, or the terrible dread she felt. The wind moaned past. She shivered and met his gaze.

"The sniper should come in from the other side on the main trail," he continued. "After that detour we forced him to take, it's the logical way for him to go."

She tilted her head and studied his face. There had to be something more that he wasn't saying, something that had put that grim determination in his eyes. "So what's the problem?"

He stuck the canteen in his pack, leveled his gaze at hers. "If I'm wrong, if he found another way around, we could be walking into an ambush. Once we enter that valley, there's no way out except up. I know the people who live in those huts," he added. "I'll ask if they've seen anyone. But he could have slipped past at night."

"So what are you thinking? That we should go around, too?"

"We could. But it will cost us a day or two."

And they'd lose their advantage of time. She flicked an uneasy gaze toward the valley again. "Then we'd better go in this way." Despite the awful dread flaying her nerves.

"You're sure? We can still go around."

She turned her gaze back to his. And she read the regret in his eyes, the concern he felt—for her. Warmth curled through her heart, and she had the sudden urge to hold him, to do something, anything to ease the torment gripping this man. How could he not realize how worthy he was? "I'm sure."

He nodded, turned away, suddenly all business again. "Once we get to the end of the valley, the trail gets steep. It's going to be dark soon, too dangerous to go up tonight. We'll camp at the base of the mountain, start up at dawn. It will take us most of the morning to climb."

He swung into the saddle, pulled her up behind him, and once she was settled, they started off. She scanned the cliffs as they entered the valley, studied the oddly shaped boulders, and shivered again. She could see why the Inca thought the place was sacred. It felt haunted, filled with ancient spirits—or death.

She shook off that dismal thought. She was being overly dramatic. The lack of sleep was affecting her mood.

But the rocks drew her gaze again and again as they plodded silently beneath them. Centuries of wind and rain had shaped and etched the stones, and they looked like snarling animals, faces of savage warriors, visions of death. She shifted closer to Logan and clutched his back, taking comfort in his strength.

Even so, she had to admit she couldn't wait to get out of the valley. The aura of evil made her skin creep.

Moments later, they arrived at the two mud huts, and Logan reined in the horse. "*Hola, buenas tardes,* Señor Mamani," he called out. His voice echoed in the gloom. "*Imaina kashanki,*" he added in Quechua.

No one answered.

She scanned the area around the huts—spotted a cone-shaped kiln, a forgotten hat and cup—and her feeling of impending doom grew. Even the horse seemed restless, his ears pinned back, swishing his tail.

"Maybe they've left, gone for supplies," she said.

Logan still watched the huts. "I smell smoke. They wouldn't have left a fire unattended."

Dara inhaled, smelled the lingering traces of smoke. He was right. She glanced past the crude mud huts, squinted at a patch of dirt surrounded by a low rock wall partway up the slope. Two alpacas watched warily from the grass nearby.

A flash of red fabric in the tilled area caught her attention, and she frowned. A bundle of blankets or something else?

"Logan," she whispered, and he glanced back. "Up there."

He looked toward the spot, and his hard jaw tensed even more. He pulled out his rifle, checked the clip. She pulled her own gun from her pack.

"Stay here," he said, his voice low. He leaped down, handed her the reins. The grooves deepened beside his mouth. He looked deadly, his eyes so intent they made her heart race. He turned to face the huts.

Tension wound through her nerves. Her sense of danger grew. She tightened her grip on her gun, sucked in a breath, adjusted the reins to quiet the horse.

Logan strode to the closest hut, kicked open the wooden door. He ducked inside, came back out a second later, then headed toward the opposite hut.

And abruptly stopped. Suddenly, she noticed a trail of dark spots near his feet. Her heart faltered. Her stomach churned even more. "Is that…"

"Yeah." He flattened his back against the low hut, military

style, then kicked open the door and charged in. Long seconds later he strode back out.

And stopped. His face had paled, his eyes turned stark.

And a chill slithered over her heart. "Are they—?"

"Yeah." His eyes met hers, and every hair on her body rose. "They're dead."

Chapter 12

Dara couldn't stop shaking.

She stood in the rocky alcove at the base of the mountain, waiting while Logan tended the horse. Bile surged in her throat. Her body was chilled. The smell of blood, the horrible stench of death still permeated her pores. And the gruesome images of death kept flickering through her head—her parents, her bodyguard, that poor Quechua family.

The man and his young son had been shot near the hut, the woman and baby murdered where they'd been digging in the field. Another spasm shuddered through her, and she closed her eyes. She tried to block out the image of the baby's sweet, round face, those darling ruddy cheeks. She panted hard, fought down the raw urge to retch.

So much death. So much senseless, tragic death. Dear God, when would it end?

She clenched her clacking teeth, opened her eyes as Logan

passed the sprawling *colli* bushes that hid the cave from the trail. He strode into the alcove, propped the gelding's packs against the rock wall.

And the guilt swarmed back, the terrible realization that he'd been right. It had been reckless to come here. She'd brought evil to those innocent people. Her selfish need to prove her worth had cost them their lives.

And now Logan was just as exposed, just as vulnerable as they had been.

He turned, braced his hands on his lean hips, and his grim gaze drove into hers. Her lungs tightened. Her eyes burned with unshed tears. "I'm so sorry," she said, and her voice cracked. "Oh, God, Logan. I never thought…I never thought…"

"Oh, hell." He strode to her, pulled her into his arms. And she leaned into him, trembling wildly, pressed her cheek to his solid chest. She was cold, so cold. She hooked her arms around his back, absorbing his heat, his massive strength.

He tucked her head beneath his chin, held her firmly against him, while one hand caressed her back. And she clung to him, seeking comfort, for the first time doubting her goal.

Was that dagger really worth this violence? Was it really worth those poor people's lives?

But if she didn't find it before that evil society did, there would be even more deaths, more innocent people killed. How could she let them win?

"We'll be all right," Logan murmured against her hair. "Nothing's going to happen to us."

"But what if we're walking into a trap? What if the killer sets up an ambush?"

"We'll be ready." His voice was firm. She knew he was trying to reassure her, and she wanted desperately to believe him. But she didn't see how they could make it up that trail.

She sucked in her breath, tried to pull herself together. She lifted her face and stepped away, but his big hand lingered on her back, as if he were reluctant to let her go. And she wanted to crawl right back into the security of his arms and forget the world.

But she'd caused this mess. Now she had to think, help him make plans. And make certain Logan survived.

She managed a wobbly smile. "I'm sorry. I don't usually fall apart."

His gaze held hers. "Violent death isn't something you get used to."

"No." She swallowed, breathed through the bile still sickening her throat, saw the stark pain haunting his eyes. And she knew those deaths had resurrected ghosts of his own.

"So what do you think?" she asked, still struggling to compose herself. "Was it the sniper?" She'd been too shocked, too horrified by the murders to take in details, but Logan had scoured the area for clues before they'd dug the graves.

"Hard to say." He turned to his pack, handed her the blankets, and she spread them on the rock floor. "There wasn't much evidence. A few 9mm casings, but that's a common round. There were footprints, mule tracks. He took their llama with him when he left."

"Their llama?" That was bizarre. Why would he need that?

Logan grunted, gathered his weapons, lowered himself to the ground. He propped a flashlight beside him, and the yellow light cut through the haze.

She wrapped herself in one of the blankets and huddled beside him, needing the comfort of human warmth.

"I didn't think the sniper could get here this fast," he added. He started taking apart his rifle, shook his head. "But he might know other trails."

She hugged her knees. "But why would the sniper murder those poor farmers? They couldn't have had anything of value." They'd barely eked out a humble existence growing potatoes and beans.

"He might not have known where the trail is. This was a sacred trail. The Inca kept it hidden. And there are a lot of blind canyons back here. You could spend weeks wandering around if you don't know where it is."

"So you think he forced that family to tell him?"

He angled his head. "It's possible. And then he didn't want to leave witnesses behind."

A deep chill scuttled down her spine. There was only one reason the sniper wouldn't want witnesses—he was planning to murder them. She inhaled the musty air of the cave, watched Logan methodically clean his gun. And a terrible feeling of impending evil slid through her.

"Is there any chance it was someone else?"

"Good question." Logan reassembled the AK-47 with a speed that stunned her. And then his gaze sliced to hers. "How much do you trust your colleague?"

"Pedro?" She frowned. "He was my academic advisor. I've known him since I was an undergrad. He's Peruvian, from Arequipa. We've worked together for years."

"Any chance he's behind this?"

She opened her mouth to protest, then hesitated. She didn't want to think her friend could betray her, but she couldn't let emotions rule her head. Not with their lives at stake.

"I don't see how," she said after a moment. "He's more interested in Quillacocha itself than the Roma dagger. He's an expert in *capacocha,* Inca sacrificial rites, and he thinks the peaks around here could yield new tombs. In fact, he'd never heard of the Roma legend until I told him. We joined forces when I figured out that the dagger was here. He helped get me access to Peruvian documents from the time of the conquest."

Logan set aside the rifle, picked up his pistol, and began to tear it down. "Then there's no rivalry?"

"Not that I've noticed. He seemed excited to help me. He's getting the permits, assembling a team to map the site. We've agreed he'll write it up. Once I have the dagger, my part is done. I never planned to hang around. I'll phone him as soon as I get to the nearest town and he'll join me there."

Logan fell silent, continued to work. She watched his hands move over the pistol with confidence, reassured by his expertise. He was as lethal as that sniper was.

"So tell me about the dagger," he finally said. "How it got to Peru."

She tugged her gaze from his hands, focused on the darkness gathering beyond the cave. The rain had held off, but thunder boomed the ground. "What do you know about the Spanish conquest?"

"Not much." He shrugged, his black hair burnished by the light. "Just the basic facts."

She snuggled deeper into the blanket, propped her chin on her knees. "It wasn't as easy as most people think. The *conquistadores,* mostly Pizarro, tried to enter Peru several times, but they only made it as far as Trujillo on the northern coast. Most of his men gave up and went back to Panama, or else they got sick and died. But Pizarro had come across some natives with gold and silver, and didn't want to quit. He kept trying to get backing for another expedition, but no one would help. They all thought it was too dangerous.

"So in 1528 he went back to Spain to get support. The queen agreed and gave him permission to proceed with the conquest. She also gave him a dagger that was rumored to have special powers. Whoever carried it was supposed to be invincible in battle."

He glanced up. "You think it was the Roma dagger?"

"The descriptions match. So does the timeline. We know

Gypsies were in Spain by then, and the crown confiscated a lot of property during the Inquisition. Plus, it explains how Pizarro could conquer Peru when his other efforts had failed."

Logan squinted down the barrel of his pistol. "There was nothing magical about it. He had better weapons—guns and horses—and he took advantage of the Incas' internal unrest. And he was ruthless, not afraid to kill."

Like the sniper.

Dara shivered again, fought back the horrific images of the slaughtered family, pulled the soft alpaca blanket tighter around her. "In any case, I think the last Inca ruler, Manco Inca, stole the dagger from Pizarro after the Spanish overthrew the empire. We know Manco Inca fled to Vilcabamba, and it was rumored that he had a special dagger that helped him survive.

"But he had treachery in his own camp. His rivals stole the dagger from him, took it to Quillacocha. I think it was buried in the last ruler's tomb.

"There isn't any proof," she admitted. "The Inca didn't have a writing system, only oral tradition. But the Spanish chroniclers and Inca *mestizos* like Garcilaso de la Vega mention it in their records. And I think the dagger's the same."

She paused. Thunder vibrated the ground again, and the deep rumble stirred up her nerves. There had been so much treachery, so much death surrounding that blade. Would they be the next to die?

She glanced at Logan, took in the ruthless set of his jaw, the harsh angles of his face lit by the flashlight's beam. He had removed his vest, and his shirt molded his powerful back.

And a chill snaked through her, a terrible sense of dread. Tomorrow they would arrive at Quillacocha. Tomorrow she would search for the sacred dagger, confront the sniper if he was there.

And tomorrow she might die.

"Logan…" She sucked in her breath, tried to quell the panic swarming her gut. "If anything happens to me tomorrow—"

"It won't." His jaw went tight.

"But…if it does…I need you to get that dagger to safety." Her eyes met his. "Promise me. My uncle will know what to do with it. Nicu Badis. He's my mother's brother. He's in San Diego now. Promise you'll get it to him."

"Listen, you're going to survive this." His gaze drove into hers, and fierce determination blazed in his eyes. And she knew with a soul-deep certainty that this man would do anything, even sacrifice his own life, to keep her safe.

Her heart tumbled, her chest swelled with emotions so powerful her hands shook. "Logan…"

"Don't worry." He set down his gun and shifted toward her, reached out and cradled her cheek. "You're going to be all right," he insisted, his deep voice rough.

Her lips trembled. She wanted to protest, tell him she wasn't worried about herself, but the words wouldn't come. She was riveted by his eyes, by the yearning rising inside her, by the raw feelings shredding her chest.

She'd had bodyguards before, men who were paid to protect her. But she'd never encountered a man like Logan Burke—a courageous, selfless man. A man willing to put his life on the line and die for her.

A true hero, no matter what he believed.

His thumb brushed her jaw, her lips. His gaze dipped, then stalled on her mouth. And that familiar urgency rose, the need to hold him, kiss him, to feel his hands on her naked skin, to give herself completely to him.

Her lips parted. Her heart beat fast. His gaze moved back to her eyes. And desire crackled between them, the same electric hunger she'd felt last night in the cave.

She moistened her lips. Dark heat flared in his eyes. And then he pulled her close, covered her mouth with his. And he kissed her with a deep, driving hunger that made her burn.

His tongue swept her mouth, exploring, arousing, possessing. As if she were his. As if he wanted to kiss her forever. And desire shocked through her, the stunning need to yield everything to this man.

But just as abruptly, he broke the kiss, and rested his forehead on hers. Her heart pulsed hard. Her ragged breath sawed with his. And then he pulled back, putting distance between them, and she saw the regret in his eyes.

"Please," she pleaded, her desperation rising. "Logan, please, I—"

"You'd better rest." He dropped his hands to his side, then gathered his weapons and rose. "We'll head out as soon as it's light."

He stalked stiffly to the edge of the cave, then turned to face her again. He stood before her like the warrior he was, a deadly weapon in each hand, his huge body dominating the space. He was hewn from muscle, honed to fight, radiating a formidable aura of power.

And his dark eyes burned with blatant male hunger, igniting a firestorm of need in her nerves. "I promise you're going to survive," he said, and then strode away.

She dropped back against the blankets, her heart slamming against her rib cage, and placed her trembling hand on her lips. Maybe she would survive this ordeal, but would her heart?

Chapter 13

The storm moved off during the night, dragging a dreary mist over the slopes. They set out in the gloom at first light, hiking single file up the steep trail. Logan led with the horse, and Dara straggled behind him, trying not to slow him down.

They'd studied her diagrams and notes before they'd left, comparing them to what Logan remembered of the ruins. And he'd reluctantly agreed that she would search the tombs while he stood guard at her back.

If they made it there alive.

She paused, sucked the cool, moist air into her burning lungs, fought the tension flaying her skull. At least the mist provided sporadic cover, making it less likely that the sniper could ambush them as they climbed. But the red rocks seemed even more sinister in the drifting fog, their savage faces snarling down at them, as if shrieking at them to turn back.

She struggled for breath, fought off the fatigue thrashing her head, hurried to catch up with the horse. They'd climbed for hours up the narrow path, winding through the forbidding rocks, past small, icy streams and haunting *haucas*—ancient shrines sculpted into the stones. Whenever the mist shifted, she caught sight of the sheer cliffs plunging on each side, and her heart quailed at the deadly drop.

Then suddenly, Rupper balked. She stopped, gasped for breath as Logan calmed the anxious horse. But the gelding tossed his head, pinned back his ears, and backed up.

"What's wrong?" she asked softly.

Logan spoke to the horse in soothing tones, patted his neck. "He senses something. I need you to hold him while I check it out."

"All right." She skirted the horse, careful not to spook him more, and took the reins. "Be careful," she whispered to Logan.

"Yeah." He pulled the pistol from his waistband, slid a round into the chamber, then vanished into the mist.

She petted the horse, felt a shiver ripple through his neck as he rolled his eyes, and her own anxiety grew. What would scare the horse? She nibbled her lip, glanced at the gray mist slithering past, shivered in the ominous chill.

"It's me," Logan warned her a moment later, and then he reappeared on the trail. He stuck his gun in his jeans, his eyes met hers, and her pulse sped up even more.

"What is it?"

"There's a dead llama up ahead. It's a fresh kill. Rupper doesn't like the smell of blood."

"You think a puma got it?"

"No." His eyes turned hard. "It was cut with a knife."

A knife? She frowned, remembered that he'd mentioned seeing llama tracks. The sniper had stolen the animal from the farmers and brought it up.

"But…why would the sniper kill it?" Surely he wouldn't take time to butcher meat if he was pursuing them.

Logan averted his eyes, shook his head. And she knew he was hiding something. Something frightening.

"There's a shortcut, a staircase ahead that comes out by the tombs," he said. "We'll leave Rupper on the trail and go up the stairs."

"All right." Logan took the lead again, and she followed, her nerves ratcheting tighter yet. The slaughtered llama creeped her out. What hadn't Logan said?

A tree emerged in the gloom, and Logan secured the horse. He loosened the cinch, made sure the gelding couldn't get tangled in the rope. Then he grabbed his rifle, shoved extra magazines in a pouch, and hefted it onto his back. She kept her own pistol close as she followed him through the mist to the steps.

And then they climbed. The steps marched up the mountain, stone after stone, hundreds of them, set methodically in place centuries ago. Dara lost count of the steps, lost track of time, just focused on continuing up. Her lungs burned and labored for air. Her thigh muscles quivered and jumped. And as the long minutes passed, her thoughts wandered from the dagger, to the llama, the sniper. To Logan's amazing kiss.

And how on earth she could convince him that he was the man she believed—the man for her.

She paused, hauled in a lungful of air, blocked off that train of thought. She couldn't worry about the future until they were safe.

And then finally, mercifully, they reached the top of the mountain. She staggered to a cluster of boulders, leaned against them and gasped for breath. She wiped her forehead on her sleeve, pressed her palm to her heaving chest. And then she turned, glimpsed the ancient city beneath the drifting mist, and her breath caught.

Quillacocha. She'd studied it, dreamed of it. And there it was at last, sprawling magically before her, a wonderland of plazas, palaces, stairways and chiseled stone walls. The thatched roofs had disintegrated long ago, leaving the buildings open to her gaze, like a stone maze seen from above.

But even ruined, the city enthralled her. Cut rocks framed open doorways. Terraces marched endlessly down the steep slopes. And in the distance she spotted the crescent-moon-shaped lake that had given the city its name.

She scanned the ancient city, the ghostly ruins, and could hardly contain her excitement. The Roma dagger was down there somewhere.

But so was the sniper.

Another chill slid through her.

Logan moved close, and his broad shoulder bumped against hers. "The tombs are over there." He pointed off to the side where the mountain cut away. "I can cover you from here. But you need to stay where the tombs are."

"All right."

"And if anything goes wrong…" His eyes met hers. "Hightail it back to Rupper and get the hell out of Peru."

She frowned, opened her mouth to protest. "Promise me, Dara," he repeated, his voice hard. "Promise you'll get yourself to safety if something goes wrong."

"All right," she said, even though she had no intention of abandoning him here. They were in this together, no matter what happened next.

She swallowed, inhaled for courage, then stepped out from behind the rock. But Logan grabbed her arm and pulled her back. "Be careful," he urged her, and his eyes burned into hers.

"I will," she whispered, gazing back. And emotions bubbled up inside her—worry, gratitude, and something more. Something too complicated to analyze now.

After several heartbeats, he finally nodded, released her arm, then propped the rifle on the rock to cover her back.

Her nerves jittering hard now, feeling completely exposed in the open, she started down the ancient stone walkway that wound through the ruins like a narrow road. She rushed past empty plazas, scurried by gaping windows cut precisely from granite blocks. The ruins were eerily silent, the only sound her footsteps slapping on rocks.

The walkway ended at the bottom of the ruins on a wide stone ledge. On one side there was nothing—only the sheer mountain dropping off. On the other was the royal mausoleum, the cave that housed the ancient tombs. She slowed, turned her attention to the mausoleum.

The stone door was open.

She stopped, eyed the granite slab that had been carelessly shoved to the side. Someone had beat her here. The sniper?

Was he still nearby? She stood frozen, listening intently, but only heard the pulse of her blood. She checked her pistol, crept to the entrance, waited for her eyes to adjust to the gloom.

And then she inhaled, burst inside. She scanned the rock-lined walls, the niches carved in the stone, and her stomach pitched. The sniper wasn't here. The musty room was empty. Too empty.

Someone had looted the graves.

Her heart ached, her mind railed against the desecration, the terrible loss to the world. She put away her pistol and pulled out her camera, snapped off several shots.

But she'd mourn the loss of the antiquities later. She had to see if the dagger was gone.

She'd discovered the reference in an obscure text, a forgotten translation of Incan folk tales by a minor seventeenth century Peruvian aristocrat. He'd discounted the story as merely a legend, wishful thinking by a defeated people about their last king's secret tomb.

Dara disagreed. She'd never seen the story mentioned else-where. And she hadn't confided the discovery to her colleagues, only guarded the information in her notes.

But if she was right, and if the looters hadn't discovered the hidden tomb...

She put the camera in her pack, slung it over her back, then turned her attention to the floor. She crept along the stones, searching carefully for the symbol that marked the spot. She quartered the space, checked inch by inch, felt her hopes begin to fade. And then she saw it.

The crescent moon.

But it wasn't on the floor. It was carved into a low stone on the farthest wall. She frowned, bit her lip. Had the story changed during the many retellings? Could the chronicler have made a mistake? There was only one way to find out.

She rushed to the stone, knelt in the dirt, fumbled for the small metal crowbar she'd carted along to pry it out. She paused to push back her hair with her sleeve, worked the crowbar under the lip of the stone, managed to catch the edge.

The stone was square, roughly two and a half feet long on each side—not huge, but also not easy to move. She tugged, managed to budge it slightly. She grunted, excited now, adjusted her grip, and pulled again. It made another small shift.

She rose to her feet, squatted to put her weight behind it, gave one big heave. The stone loosened, then toppled to the floor with a heavy thump, barely missing her foot. She quickly scooted out of the way.

And then she gaped at the small, open space. Cool, dank air wafted out.

She'd found the secret tomb.

Her heart went berserk with the thrill of discovery. Her breath came in fast, shallow gasps. Moving quickly, she wriggled through the opening into the dimly lit space.

Then froze.

Straight ahead on a low stone slab, sat a mummy. He was huddled in the fetal position, his face covered with a golden death mask, his skeleton wrapped in a beautiful, ancient cloth shot with gold. Huge gold plates, adorned with symbols of the sun god Inti lined the slab and walls. And beside him lay a golden bowl filled with coca leaves, a pair of woven shoes—and a dagger. The Roma dagger.

Her heart stopped.

Her hands trembled. She whipped out her camera, began snapping photos, only pausing to stare. This was amazing, a discovery that would rock the world. She was the first person to see the inside of this tomb in five hundred years.

She knew she should have a team with her, permits. Her conscience rebelled at disturbing the site, moving anything before the proper documentation was done. But she didn't dare leave the dagger here, not with that sniper so close. She'd just have to record where she'd found it, and avoid disturbing anything else.

Her heart hammering, her throat so dry she couldn't swallow, she took photo after photo from every angle she could. Then she set down the camera, grabbed the sketchpad from her bag, and quickly outlined the tomb. Her colleague, Pedro, would take measurements once he arrived, but she wanted to document as much as she could.

That done, she reverently approached the mummy. She muttered a prayer under her breath, not knowing what ancient spirits guarded the place. But she could feel them. The air vibrated with unseen power, like a deep humming swelling up from the earth. The hairs rose on the nape of her neck.

Her hands shaking, she reached out and picked up the dagger. It was over a foot long, heavier than she'd expected. The leather scabbard was intricately tooled, beaded with gold and silver threads in sacred Roma designs.

She slowly extracted the blade, and her breath caught. The hilt was made of a pure orange gold, encrusted with amber in every shade—blue, green, a dazzling deep blood red. Roma symbols were carved around the gems—the sun, the serpent, the crescent moon. The steel blade glimmered in the dim light, its famous wootz pattern like damask silk. The blade was incised with grooved channels—blood channels—a grim reminder of its deadly use.

And she could feel the power in it, the energy that buzzed through her hands. She shivered, slid it back into the scabbard. Generations of her ancestors had fought with this blade, killed with it.

Died for it.

She prayed she wouldn't be next.

An urgency gripped her, a sudden need to get out fast. She placed the dagger in her pack, scurried out of the secret tomb, rolled the perfectly cut stone back into place.

And then she rushed from the mausoleum, into the swirling mist.

Just as a shot rang out.

Chapter 14

The gunshot whined through the ruins, the sharp report echoing through the mountains again and again. Dara froze, every muscle cemented in place, unable to draw in a breath.

Who had fired? Had the sniper shot at Logan? Logan at him? Or had that bullet been aimed at her?

Fear streaked through her like the sizzle of lightning, spurring her into action, and she lunged toward the cave's outer wall. She plastered herself against the rocks, her heart rocketing, trying to keep from being seen.

Her pulse slammed against her skull. Stark fear mauled her chest. The echo faded, and a terrible silence rose in the air, swelling, suffocating. Nothing moved. She didn't breathe. Even the mist hung still, as if waiting, waiting…

Logan would have called out if he'd shot the sniper. He would have told her that he was all right.

Which meant that sniper was still alive.

But was Logan?

She wheezed in air, beat back the awful dread. Logan wasn't hurt. He couldn't be hurt. That sniper couldn't win.

She tugged her gun from her bag, tried to plan through the panic hazing her brain. She had to get back up the hill to Logan. She didn't dare climb straight up the walkway; she'd be too exposed. But Logan had warned her not to leave this part of the ruins. She'd be out of his sight, beyond his help.

If he was even alive.

She shoved that doubt from her mind, focused on what to do. Her only option was to zigzag back through the ruins, sticking as close to the walkway as she could—and pray that the sniper didn't spot her before she reached the top.

She inched along the wall of the cave to the narrow walkway, so scared she could hardly breathe. Then she rushed out into the open, raced up several stone steps. She reached a ruined building, darted inside, ducked behind the rock wall.

Her heart hammered fast. Her breath came in quick, shallow gasps. She covered her mouth with her hand, tried not to breathe too loudly and give her location away.

A few seconds later, she crept through the room to the opposite doorway, staying as close to the wall as she could. Except for the tombs, which were in caves, none of the buildings had roofs—which made her visible from above.

Like a mouse scurrying through a maze.

And the sniper could be up there watching.

Her dread rising, she peeked out the doorway, took advantage of the drifting mist to dash up a dozen more steps. But instead of reaching another building, there was only an open plaza, nothing she could hide behind. Desperate, she dove behind a low stone bench.

Ignoring the pebbles digging into her knees, she crawled along the ground behind the bench, praying it would shield her from view. But then her foot struck a stone, and it tumbled behind her, thudding like gunfire in the quiet gloom. She stopped, petrified, and didn't breathe. Had the sniper heard that? Did he now know where she was?

Her belly turned to ice.

But she couldn't stop, couldn't succumb to the fear. She had to block out the panic, focus, concentrate on getting back up that hill.

She spotted a building ahead, rose from her crouch, and raced across the plaza to the open door. Inside, she paused, glanced around at the chiseled granite, searching for a better way out. But a trail of dark splotches stained the rock floor.

Blood. Fresh blood.

Her lungs stopped. She stood rigid, paralyzed with dread. Was Logan injured? Was that his blood?

She had to find out. Trembling, her blood rushing in her ears, she swallowed and followed the drips to a huge, flat stone several yards away. And then she gasped.

There was a bloody lump on the stone.

The llama's entrails?

She recoiled. Bile rose in her throat. She gagged, clamped her palm over her mouth, fought back the urge to retch.

Horrified, trying not to inhale the coppery stench of blood, she forced herself to inch close. Next to the llama's remains was a design painted in blood. A crescent moon with an evil slash.

The symbol of the secret society—the Order of the Black Crescent Moon.

Blinded by panic, she whirled, bolted back through the open door. She raced across the walkway, rushed wildly through another building, sprinted up several more stairs. Frenzied, desperate to get away, she darted from room to room. She zigzagged through buildings, crossed plazas, running faster, harder, heedless of the noise she made, until she neared the top of the hill.

She stopped, braced herself against a stone wall. Enough! She had to stop, calm down, think! She was almost to the end of the walkway, to the boulder where Logan was. Panicking now could get him killed.

Taking a firm hold on her nerves, trying to block out thoughts of the llama, she dragged in another breath. Then she crept back to the open doorway, eyed the last cluster of buildings that branched off the path. Hysteria spiraled inside her. It was like a madhouse. Which room held the sniper? Which room should she go in?

Or was the sniper waiting above her? Had he been toying with her all this time, snickering, just watching, watching…

She shook off the doubts, then sprinted up the last few steps. She veered into a random room, paused, and glanced around. *Empty.* Her breath rushed out in relief.

But now she had to find Logan.

She hurried to a large window that looked out over the slope. Only a few feet from the building, the mountain sheered off in a dizzying drop. She flicked her gaze uphill, spotted the boulder where Logan had been standing guard. He wasn't there. Or at least she couldn't see him. She leaned out farther, spotted him creeping around another rock a short distance away.

Relief flooded through her. He was alive. Thank God! She wanted to call out, tell him where she was, but then the sniper would know.

Suddenly, only a few yards from where she stood, a man snaked into view, his body hugging the ground. She blinked, stared. From hood to boots, he was covered with dirt and dried grass, blending in perfectly with the terrain. Only the sleek, deadly rifle in his hands betrayed who he was.

The sniper.

He rose, crouched behind a low stone retaining wall, his back to her. Then he raised his rifle, took aim at Logan.

Panic seized her. The hair at her nape stood on end. "Logan," she screamed. "Watch out!"

Logan dove behind the rock. The sniper whirled toward her and fired. The shot hit the wall beside her head, deafening her with the blast. She raised her own gun and squeezed the trigger, but nothing happened. Her gun had jammed!

Shocked, she ducked back inside the building. Her breath came in fast, harsh pants. There was no time to run. He would reach the window in seconds, shoot her before she crossed the room. She was trapped.

The hell she was.

Fury rushed through her, a cold, savage haze of rage. She wasn't going to die like this. She wasn't going to let him kill her, kill Logan, steal the dagger for his sick, twisted ends.

She dropped her gun and grabbed a rock, then forced herself to wait. Her vision narrowed. Time seemed to slow.

Then she heard it—a slight, muffled step just outside the wall. She lunged up, turned, and heaved the rock out the window with all her might. It smashed into the sniper's shoulder, catching him by surprise. He staggered back, shook his head, raised his rifle to fire.

But he'd stepped too far back, too close to the edge of the slope. He tottered back. His arms flailed. His gun fired into the air. His eyes fastened on hers, filled with shock, disbelief.

And then he plunged back into the chasm. Dara screamed, clamped her hand over her mouth, horrified by the sight. He'd fallen. She'd killed him. Oh, God. She'd actually killed a man.

She squeezed her eyes shut, tried to block out the ghastly thought, that he would slam to the ground below. She waited, not wanting to listen, while a terrible, aching silence throbbed in her ears.

Then she heard footsteps, opened her eyes. Logan ran to the edge of the cliff, peered down, his rifle aimed. After a moment, he lowered the gun. "He's gone."

She stood rooted, unable to move. She just stared at the cliff, trembling, her legs quivering like a leaf in a storm. She'd never killed anyone before, never had to, never wanted to.

But he'd been trying to kill Logan, kill her people, kill her.

Logan strode to the window, hoisted himself inside. He set down his weapon, then pulled her into his arms. And she buried her face in his chest, shivering at the horror of it, the terrible violence of it, that they nearly hadn't survived.

"It's over," Logan murmured. He cradled her head, rocked with her, rubbed her back, and all she could do was hold him, hold him. She'd almost lost him. She closed her eyes, felt the solid, safe, masculine strength of him, never wanted to let him go.

And he held her just as tightly, pressing her head to his chest, his jaw to her cheek, as if to convince himself she was alive.

After an eternity, he eased his head back, lifted her chin, and his eyes burned into hers. His dark, carnal eyes.

Her pulse ran hot. Her breath wedged in her throat. And his sexual appeal washed over her, the fierce, primal masculinity of this man.

He brushed his knuckles along her jaw, slid his mouth over hers. His lips were warm, gentle, and she knew he meant the kiss as comfort. But the thrilling feel of him scorched through her blood, sparking a need inside her—the need to feel, to live, to celebrate being alive in the face of death.

But he pulled away before she could respond. "You got the dagger?" he asked, his voice rough.

"Yes."

"Good. Then let's get out of here. This place gives me the creeps."

She glanced at the cliff through the window again and trembled hard. He was right. This wasn't the place to linger.

But as she followed him out the doorway and up the worn, stone steps of the ancient ruins, a new thought jolted her heart. Their journey was nearly over. She'd found the blade, had no reason to stay in Peru. Logan would take her to the nearest town, and then he would go.

But she'd learned something on this trip. Life was short, far too short to waste. Her parents' murders and the deaths she'd seen in Peru had driven that point home.

And she loved this man. She blinked at the realization. It was true. She really did love him. She loved his courage, his code of honor, the ruthless way he protected her. And no matter what he thought, he was her destined mate.

So tonight, she was going to prove it. She was going to break through his barriers, show him how much she cared. She eyed the rugged strength of his back, the primitive power in his strides.

And a heady thrill rushed through her. Tonight she was going to make love to Logan Burke.

He'd almost lost her. He'd almost failed her. Dara had nearly died.

Logan sat near the campfire he'd built, still unable to shake off the fear. They'd hiked back down the mountain to retrieve the gelding, found the sniper's mule hobbled near the main trail. They'd set up camp, made dinner, even washed in a mountain stream. And he still kept reliving that terrible moment when he'd seen the sniper aim his rifle at her.

He'd never been more terrified in his life.

But Dara had saved herself. Saved him. The image of her hurling that rock at the sniper was etched in his brain. What a courageous woman.

His brave and amazing princess.

Not his, he reminded himself grimly. She could never be his. And now that she'd found the dagger, she would leave.

Still trying to convince himself the danger was over, he picked up the ancient dagger, and hefted it in his hands. The light from the campfire mingled with the full moon rising over the mountains and glimmered off the golden hilt. He examined the thick, leather scabbard, the intricate beadwork tooled in exotic designs, then clasped the dagger's hilt. It fit perfectly in his hand.

He tugged on the scabbard. The blade slid free with a lethal hiss—fifteen inches of deadly steel. The same steel that had terrified the medieval crusaders, been rumored to slice through armor and rock. Steel forged by expert craftsmen in an ancient art now lost. He tested the gleaming blade with his thumb, drew a drop of blood. Still sharp after a thousand years.

He flicked his wrist, slashed at the air, marveling at the balance, the power in the blade. He was a man grounded in reality—stark, harsh reality. But the energy in the blade, the power singing through the steel tempted him to believe—that maybe magic did exist, that maybe this dagger did have special powers.

A small sound came from the periphery of the campfire, and he glanced up. Dara crept into the golden light, clutching a long blanket around her.

She stood there for a moment, gazing at the fire, and the startling beauty of her swept through his nerves. Those dark, exotic eyes. That shimmering curtain of hair. The sultry allure of those full, lush lips.

And the memories flashed back—her glimmering thighs, her naked breasts, her nipples swelling and pouting for his kiss. The erotic images whipped through his brain, making his body grow taut, his blood buzz loud in his skull.

His gaze stayed riveted on her as she quietly strolled to his side. She knelt beside him, and her feminine scent drifted over him, making his heart beat loud, the blood turn thick in his veins. She tugged the blanket closer around her, stared at the fire, and his hands trembled with the need to reach for her, stroke the curve of her cheek, her throat, plunge his hands through that silken hair.

The need swelled, pounded through his loins. And thousands of years of biology surged inside him, urging him to claim her, take her. The need was as ancient as man, an aftermath of the violence searing his blood. The urge was primitive, compelling, nearly overwhelming.

But she wasn't his to take. The irony of that made his mouth twist. She was perfect for him, the only woman he'd ever craved.

And she was completely taboo.

With great difficulty, he dragged his gaze back to the blade, then inhaled to cool his blood. The scent of smoke from the burning brush merged with the crisp night air.

"So what do you think about the dagger?" she asked, and her low, sultry voice pulsed through his nerves.

He kept his eyes on the blade, turned it, and the steel blazed and danced in the light. "It's one hell of a blade," he admitted. "I've never seen anything like it."

Her eyes latched on his. "Do you feel the…power in it?"

"Yeah, I feel it." The current vibrated through the blade, magical, deadly. He slid the dagger back into its sheath, and handed it to her. "What will you do with it now?"

She pulled a T-shirt from her backpack, wrapped the dagger carefully in the cloth. "I'll turn it over to the international group that's guarding the necklace. It's the only way to keep it safe."

"What about the other treasure—the crown? Will you look for that?"

"I doubt it." She shook her head. "I don't have any idea where it is."

She placed the dagger in her backpack, set it aside. Then she pulled her knees to her chin, turned her face to the moon, and her long hair tumbled down her back. "According to the legend, when all three treasures are finally united, the true Roma leader will be revealed. There'll be a sign, a blood-red lunar eclipse. And then the Roma will regain their power, their homeland."

He glanced at the full moon rising above the hills. Its haunting face stared back at him, secretive, omniscient, as if it really could foretell fate. He shook off the fanciful thought. "Do you believe it?"

She sighed. "No, not really. My parents worked for peace in Romanistan for years before they were exiled. The politics are complicated. Too many factions want power. And now that they've discovered oil…"

She shook her head. "But the people believe in the legend. This dagger is a symbol for them. It will give them hope, the strength to fight back against prejudice and injustice, even if they are scattered around the world."

Logan nodded, dropped his gaze to the fire. And for a long moment, neither spoke. Small rustlings arose from the nearby grass—wild rabbits, *cuy*. Several yards off, the gelding and mule stirred and stamped their hooves.

And he watched the play of the flames, the way the deadly heat dueled and danced. Then Dara inched closer beside him. Too close. Her shoulder brushed his. He inhaled her sweet, earthy scent. He turned his head, and her eyes lifted to his.

She wanted him.

The awareness flashed through him, like an electric zap to his blood.

He didn't move.

His heart sped up. Hunger drummed in the air. And the desire in her eyes kept him paralyzed, unable to breathe.

Her tongue swept her lips, and the slow, erotic motion

riveted his gaze. His throat grew dry. The blood rushed from his head. He dragged his eyes back to hers.

"Logan," she whispered in her throaty voice, and he was instantly, vibrantly aroused.

"We can't do this." The words came out husky, tormented.

"We can." She rose, kneeled before him, locked her hands behind his neck.

He groaned, balled his hands to keep from touching her. "Dara, stop. You're the princess. A virgin. You can't just—"

"I'm a woman, only a woman." Her dark eyes melted into his. "Logan, please." Desperation seeped into her voice. "I need you."

The blanket slid loose, and his gaze followed, making a slow, hot slide to her breasts. Her full, heavy breasts. Her T-shirt was snug; her nipples pebbled against the fabric, as if waiting, begging for his touch. His body went hot and taut.

He closed his eyes, battling the need. But she moved closer, straddling his legs with hers, the lush feel of her scrambling his brain. His hands gripped her hips of their own accord.

He could have lifted her up, set her aside. She was no match for his strength, and they both knew it. But the smell of this soft, willing woman demolished his nerves. And the need that had been brewing inside him whipped violently to life.

They'd nearly died today. But they'd survived. And everything male in him urged him to celebrate life in man's most basic, primitive way.

With Dara.

He opened his eyes, snared by the desire, the need in her eyes. He'd be damned if he did, tortured forever if he didn't.

He lowered his mouth to hers, and surrendered to his doom.

Chapter 15

He mouth was heaven—total, erotic bliss. Logan sank into the kiss, slanting his mouth over hers, giving in to the need that had tormented him for days. He plunged his hands into her hair, bunched that thick, silky mass in his fists, while he ravished her mouth with his tongue.

She was exquisite. Perfect. The taste of her flooded his senses, ignited a rush of heat in his blood, and he knew he'd never get enough. He'd thirsted for this woman since the moment he'd seen her. She'd become an obsession, an ache that refused to subside.

He deepened the kiss, slid one hand to her jaw, her throat, savoring the velvet of her skin. She was so smooth, so soft, so sultry. And her moist, warm lips drew him relentlessly in, luring him deeper, deeper into her fire.

She moved against him, stroking his shoulders, his back. She tightened her hands around his neck, and the motion pressed her breasts against his chest. Hunger drummed through his veins. He made a low, deep growl against her mouth.

And she moaned back, a sweet sound of sensual surrender that scorched through his blood.

He wanted to rip the clothes from her skin, slake the fierce need battering his loins. The urgency slammed through his nerves with a primitive violence that caught him off guard. But she was a virgin. He had to slow down, make this perfect for her.

Calling on all his self-control, he beat back the unruly need, eased himself back from the edge. He gentled the kiss, tugging her in deeper, seducing her with long, drugging sweeps of his tongue. And she yielded to him, giving herself over for his pleasure, like every fantasy he'd ever had.

Unable to stand the torment, needing to get closer, he broke the kiss and rose, tugging her to her feet. He lowered his hands to her hips, pulled her against his arousal, torturing himself, and showing her exactly how ready he was.

Her head fell back, exposing the long, creamy line of her throat. And he seared a path up that smooth, satin skin, kissing along her jaw, her cheek, her mouth.

She shuddered against his lips. The sound incinerated his nerves.

He plundered her mouth without restraint then, in a raw, savage kiss that razed his self-control. He kept one big hand on her lush bottom, riveting her where he needed her most, and slid the other beneath her shirt. The feel of her bare skin ripped through his senses, and he swept his trembling hand to her breast. She wasn't wearing a bra.

His body bucked, jolted hard. He broke the kiss, stripped off her T-shirt in one quick motion, and then stepped slightly away.

She stood before him in the moonlight, a vision of beauty, like an ancient goddess, all gleaming skin and provocative curves. His gaze swept her elegant face, to the long black hair spilling over her shoulders, over the mesmerizing swell of her breasts. The firelight danced behind her, bathing her skin in a golden glow. And her nipples tilted up, beckoning him, inviting his mouth, his touch.

His blood whipped through his skull. Every muscle in his body turned hard. He stepped forward and gently, reverently cupped her breasts with his hands, lowered his head, laved the delicate tips with his tongue.

She moaned and grasped his head.

For an eternity, he couldn't pull away. He was lost in the delirium of her skin, her breasts, in desire so intense that his hands shook. He'd never seen a woman more alluring, more enthralling. She was every dream he'd ever had.

But finally, he forced up his head. Her eyes were dazed, her body trembling for him. And his own need bludgeoned his gut. "I need to see all of you, Dara." His voice came out thick, hoarse.

She stepped back, pulled off her boots and socks while he stripped off his own shirt. And then her eyes met his. She reached for the snap on her jeans, then paused.

Her gaze darkened. Hunger screamed in the air.

She undid the snap, and the slight sound ripped through the night.

And then she slowly peeled her jeans down her thighs, kicked them aside.

Her legs glimmered in the firelight, sleek and taut and long, a paradise of sensuous curves. He couldn't move. He stood riveted by the sight of those legs, by the dark hair beckoning beneath the scrap of silk, unable to draw in a breath.

Then she shimmied the remaining barrier from her skin, let it drop. And she stood before him in total naked glory, the most erotic vision he'd ever seen.

For a long moment, he stood immobile, just drinking in the

sight of her, memorizing every swell. He couldn't swallow around the thickness blocking his throat.

But then he tore off his own remaining clothes and stood before her, watching her devour him with her eyes. He knew he couldn't rush her, but he thrummed beneath her visual exploration, every part of him clenched.

Her low, husky sigh pierced the night.

Unable to hold off any longer, he reached for her. He ran his hands over her hips, her back, kissing her shoulder, her neck, the alluring hollow of her throat. And she stroked him, approved of him with her soft, gentle hand, like an ancient princess giving benediction to her knight.

Humbled, awed by this woman, he closed his eyes. She'd trusted him to protect her, saved his life by risking her own. And now she'd bared her body to him as she'd done for no other man. She was offering him her virginity, her most precious gift, as if he were her worthy mate. Feelings swelled in his chest, crowded his throat, powerful emotions he couldn't name.

But he could give her pleasure she wouldn't forget.

He reached out, snagged her wrist to stop the torture, and gazed into those smoldering eyes. "Do you know how often I've thought of this?" he asked, and his voice sounded dredged from the earth. "Day and night. Every damned minute since you walked into that bar. I've burned for you. I've wanted to strip off your clothes and touch you, just like this."

Surprise flared in her eyes, merged into heat as he stroked his palm up her thigh. He kept his gaze locked on hers, snaring her, as he brushed her most sensitive skin. Her breath hitched. Her body trembled. Her eyes turned limpid with need.

He took her mouth in a savage, fiery kiss that left no doubt about his desire. And his hands kept stroking her thighs, kneading the beautiful globes of her bottom, slipping into and over her core.

His mouth inched from hers, down the line of her throat. Her low moan broke through the night.

"And I've wanted to lay with you." He was shaking now, desperate to slake the need that was driving him hard. "Lay down with me, Dara. Let me have you, all of you."

He pulled her to her knees, lowered her gently to the blanket, and aligned his body to hers. He braced his weight on his forearms, then returned his mouth to hers, no longer coaxing, but conquering, invading.

And she wrapped her arms around his neck, kissed him back with an urgency that matched his own. He devoured her, committing each ripe, creamy swell of her to his memory, worshipping her with his hands, his mouth.

He edged her legs apart with his knees, rose above her, his body pulsing with need. And then he looked at her. She lay trapped in his gaze, open to him, her eyes dark and unfocused, her full lips parted, swollen from his kiss. Her scent drenched his brain, fogged his mind. And every masculine instinct urged him to plunder, take what was clearly his.

He paused, spread her legs even farther apart, then stroked over her moist heat with his swollen length, allowing himself just the slightest feel of her silk.

His body went rigid. He trembled and fought for control. He wanted to claim her, drive into her with deep and total possession, satisfy the hunger that burned in his blood.

But she'd never lain with any man. He would be the first. He wanted to be the last and make her his.

He bracketed her head with his hands, slid his mouth down her temple, her cheek, raining kisses along her jaw, her eyes. And emotions surged inside him, feelings he had no right to feel. Tenderness, possession.

"Dara," he pleaded, not even knowing what he asked.

She stroked his rough jaw, and her dark fringed gaze held his.

And the absolute trust in her eyes rocked his heart. This woman, this beautiful woman who could have any man, wanted *him*. And she trusted him to be the honorable, heroic man she believed.

And even as his blood roared, even as his primitive instincts struggled to beat out the sanity, drowning him with the urgent need to mate, he knew he couldn't disappoint her. He could never dishonor this woman. He couldn't fail her in this fundamental way.

Her people had rules, strict rules. He might not agree with them, but he couldn't break them and then leave her to pay the price.

She might think she didn't care. Her body wept for him right now. Her ripe, feminine body was primed for him, needed him, with a desperation he could feel.

But he'd seen his mother's pain at being shunned, watched the shame destroy her life. And he could never do that to this woman, no matter how urgently, how desperately, he ached for her now.

He kissed her, unable to disguise the emotions inside him, his body surging out of control. And then he rested his forehead against hers.

"Stay with me," he ground out. And then he reached down and stroked her with his hand. He circled the swollen bud, dipped into her wetness, teasing her, until she moved against his hand.

"Look at me," he growled, and her eyes jerked to his.

Her eyes were glazed, mindless with hunger. Her lips were parted, her skin glistening with sweat.

And his heart swelled with pride, fierce possessiveness. He stroked and fondled her relentlessly, wrenching her higher and higher, until she thrashed, begging him, her body beyond her control. Her feminine scent filled his skull.

And then she shattered, came apart with a violent tremor. He stifled her scream with his lips, plundered her mouth with his tongue, showing her what his body ached to do.

What he could never do.

Endless moments later, her shudders ebbed into tiny tremors. And he kissed her eyelids, her forehead, her face, then slowly pulled away from her, so aroused he could hardly breathe.

And he saw the confusion enter her eyes, the hurt. "Logan, what's wrong? Why didn't you—"

"Shh." He brushed her cheek with his thumb, caressed the soft curve of her lower lip, wanting her so badly his hands shook. "I can't take your virginity and shame you. Don't ask me to do it, darlin'."

What they'd done was already outrageous, especially for the Roma princess. Her kin could kill him for even this. But he'd left her a virgin. Unless she revealed what they'd done, no man would ever know.

The thought that any other man would see her like this— her skin naked and flushed, her flesh swollen and hot—filled him with rush of violence so intense that his blood boiled. He'd kill anyone who tried.

He closed his eyes, sucked in his breath, struggled to cool the need from his veins. She wasn't his!

He wished she could be. He wished he could be the man she believed. But there was no magic that could erase the past.

He blew out his breath, opened his eyes, let his gaze take one last slide over her body, filling his memory with every glorious inch of her skin. The beauty of her robbed his breath.

And then he did the most difficult thing he'd ever done. He rose, stalked stiffly away from her into the darkness.

Where he belonged.

The flames of the campfire twisted and lunged, colliding in vibrant streams of heat. Dara huddled near the flames and watched them burn, just as she had in Logan's arms. She burrowed deeper into the blanket, her mind in turmoil, remnants of that fiery pleasure still singeing her blood.

He'd been incredible, the pleasure delirious, so raw it merged into pain. She drew in a breath, and she could still smell the musk of his skin, the heady scent of his body on hers.

She closed her eyes, letting the memories blaze through her—the stark need in Logan's eyes, his muscles bunching and flexing beneath her hands. The devastating power of his kiss.

But it hadn't been enough. She trembled, opened her eyes, returned her gaze to the fire. She'd been desperate to feel him inside her, to have him complete her, to be the first, the last, the *one*.

He strode into view then, carrying the sniper's pack, and her gaze roved helplessly over him—the rugged face that made her breath catch, the compelling strength of his arms. He dropped the pack and lowered himself to the ground beside her, not too close, not quite meeting her gaze. She eyed the powerful ledge of his shoulders, the jaw set in that familiar, implacable line, felt his restless male energy ripple the air.

He'd been careful to keep his distance since she'd come undone in his arms. There was an edginess boiling beneath his surface, as if he had a tenuous grip on his control.

And when his eyes met hers, they burned.

She watched him rifle through the pack, examine the sniper's handguns with an expertise that both impressed and disturbed her. He'd once again become the lethal warrior, walling himself off from the world.

And it struck her that there was something terribly lonely, something desolate about his ruthless self-control. As if he'd exiled his heart and locked her out.

She watched him handle the guns, shivered at the memory of those callused fingers on her skin. She understood why he hadn't taken her virginity. His honor ran too deep. He'd seen his mother suffer, took the blame for failing his wife. And she'd rather rip out her heart than cause him more pain.

But how could she heal him if he wouldn't let her get close?

"We can reach San Felipe in two or three days," he said suddenly. "You can call your colleague from there."

Two days? "So soon?" She stared at him, aghast.

"Depending on the condition of the path. We'll follow the main Inca trail down the mountain. It will take us close."

She nodded, tore her gaze away, and a hollow pit formed in her gut. Of course, she couldn't linger here. She'd found the dagger, now she had to get it to safety fast. And she couldn't shirk her responsibility to her people, no matter what her heart yearned to do.

But that meant her time with Logan was nearly over.

She stared at the fire, her thoughts and emotions in sudden turmoil. Maybe Logan was anxious to see her go. Maybe it was presumptuous to think he'd want her to stay. He'd never mentioned his feelings, only the lust.

No, he had feelings for her. She'd felt them. This wounded, complicated man cared. But how much?

Maybe it was time to find out.

Her stomach pitched. Nerves swarmed into her throat. She met his gaze, held her breath. "You could come with me…back to the States."

He stilled, then closed his eyes. "Dara, don't." His voice was low, filled with regret, and her heart made a painful lurch.

"But why not?" Desperation threaded her voice. "You could help me, help the people. I want you to come. I…need you."

"I can't. Just leave it at that, all right?"

"But—"

"Dara, come on. Be realistic."

"I am being realistic."

"You're a princess." He shook his head. "You're completely out of my league."

She stared at him, at this gorgeous, sexy man who thrilled

her in every way. "That's crazy. How can you say that? You're the most courageous, most amazing man I know."

He made a sound of disgust. "I'm an uneducated mountain tracker. I never finished high school."

"Only because your mother—"

"It doesn't matter why. You're an archeologist. You've got a Ph.D."

"So?" She lifted her hand. "That doesn't mean anything."

"It matters." The planes of his face turned grim. "We've got nothing in common. And I already had one marriage like that. I won't relive that hell."

"But we do have things in common."

"Like what?" A cynical look filled his eyes. "Look around you. This is my life. I've never even worn a suit. Can you see me going to fancy dinners? Attending receptions and balls?"

Her temper flared. How dare he sell himself short? "Yes, I can. You'd fit in anywhere. And it's not like my life's so elegant. I live in an apartment, not a palace. There isn't a kingdom anymore. Any land we had in Romanistan we lost a thousand years ago. And the Roma are divided, spread throughout the world. I don't have any real authority, no power over anyone. I'm just a symbol, a figurehead."

"Exactly. You're their leader." He leveled his gaze at hers. "And your people would never accept me. I'm only half Roma, illegitimate. My mother was shunned by her clan. No way am I worthy of a princess."

"You're wrong. They would accept you." She lifted her chin. "And even if they didn't, it wouldn't matter. I know you're worthy. You've got courage, honor, strength. And anyone who meets you will know it, too."

He stood, lifted the pack, his eyes suddenly looking dangerous. His voice turned lethal and low. "You don't know me. Don't make me into something I'm not."

"I know what matters." She rose, stepped toward him, un-willing to let him go.

But he leaned toward her, halting her steps, and his eyes turned fiercer yet. "Then *know* this, Dara. I *wanted* my wife to leave me. I was *glad* when she rode away. Relieved. I wanted her out of my sight."

The fury in his voice, the self-loathing stopped her cold. And her anger abruptly fled.

The veins stood out in his neck. His eyes were black with pain. Her chest tightened, her heart wrenched for this anguished man.

She stepped to him, placed her hand on his steely bicep, her throat so thick she could barely speak. "But you didn't want her to die," she whispered. "That part wasn't your fault."

"It doesn't matter." He stepped back, moved away from her hand.

She inhaled, struggled to get air around the fierce ache lodged in her throat, and her desperation surged. She couldn't let him retreat behind his walls. She'd lose him forever unless she reached him now. "Logan, please." Her voice quavered. "Come with me. I love you."

He stiffened. His eyes went blank, his face wooden. And the words lingered in the air between them. Stark. Awkward. Un-welcome.

Then he closed his eyes and exhaled, as if to spare her the rejection she'd see in his eyes. Her stomach churned, her heart twisted with an ache so sharp that she clutched her chest.

His eyes opened, filled with regrets. "I told you from the start. I can't be the man you need."

He turned, strode away. And she watched him go, her hopes shredding, an unbearable longing sweeping her heart.

"You're wrong," she whispered. "You're exactly the man I need."

But now she had to let him go.

Chapter 16

What a fiasco this had turned into.

Logan exhaled, ran his hand down Rupper's foreleg, signaling the gelding to lift his hoof. He didn't believe for a minute that Dara loved him. The adrenaline rush of the past few days, the fear of seeing those farmers killed had knocked her emotions off track. Once she got back to her normal life, she'd forget him, find a more appropriate—more deserving—man.

Scowling, he ran the pick around the gelding's hoof. He didn't want her to find another man. He wanted her for himself. That much was clear. He'd tossed and turned the entire night, aching to go to her, tortured by the scent of her, hungering to claim her as his.

But he couldn't have her. That was even more obvious. And the sooner he took her down the mountain and got himself out of her life, the better off they'd both be.

He straightened, glanced at her as she stood petting the

sniper's mule. The mist had returned overnight, blanketing the mountain in a muffled gloom, and moisture beaded her hair. His gaze swept the full, high breasts filling out her sweatshirt, the perfect flare of her hips, the way her lips pouted as she stroked the mule.

And suddenly, he knew with a bone-deep certainty that no matter how many years went by, he would never get her out of his blood.

His throat tightened. He pulled his eyes back to his horse, tested the cinch, while a hollow feeling seeped through his chest. He'd suffer the loss of her forever, all right. But that was his problem, not hers.

Forcing his attention back to his job, he strode to the mule, checked to make sure the packs were balanced and wouldn't slip. The sniper's mule had turned out to be docile, steady, about thirteen hands tall, a good size for Dara to ride.

"I shortened the stirrups for you," he said.

"Thanks." She pulled out her bottle of water, and took a sip. He gave the mule's pack a final tug, glanced at her again. A stray drop of water slid down her jaw, and he stilled, mesmerized by it, paralyzed by the sudden urge to lick it from her skin.

She swallowed, wiped her mouth on her hand. Her gaze collided with his.

His heart beat fast. The air turned too stuffy to breathe. His mind flashed to how she'd looked in the firelight, her bare skin flushed, her eyes dazed and pleading, her flesh swollen and aching for him.

He worked his jaw, jerked his eyes back to the mule. And then he just stood there, his pulse thundering, overwhelmed by the raw need battering his blood. It took several seconds before he could remember where he was.

She cleared her throat. "You never said what you found in

the sniper's packs." Her voice came out low, husky, and his blood made a heavy surge.

He hauled the damp air into his lungs, forced his mind from the need. "Weapons, a bedroll. Not much else. He packed light."

"Any idea who he was?"

"Ramón Gutierrez, according to his passport. You recognize the name?"

She shook her head, and he shrugged. "The passport's probably fake." He scooted past her, careful not to touch her or inhale her scent, then held the reins while she mounted the mule.

"I left it in the pack with the weapons," he added. "We'll turn it over to the police when we get to town." He stepped back, made sure her feet hung right in the stirrups, then swung himself onto his horse.

And he knew that unless he got a grip, got the hunger under control, this would be a torturous trip. Even looking at her made him want to crowd her against the nearest tree and ease his lust.

He nudged Rupper into a walk, determined to divert his thoughts. "What do you know about that secret society?"

"Aside from the fact that they murdered my parents?" Her lips tightened, and sudden pain slashed her eyes. "Not that much, really. No one knows how many members there are, only that they're spread around the world. They have a king who claims he's descended from the ancient Sumerians. He thinks he's the rightful owner of the Roma treasures, not us.

"The rest of the members are either foot soldiers or knights. The knights are the ones with the tattoo." Her eyes met his. "I didn't tell you, but the sniper left their symbol in the ruins."

"The crescent moon?"

"Yes." She shuddered, shot a worried glance toward the ruins. "He painted it on an altar. In blood."

Logan's gut chilled, and he was suddenly damned glad that the sniper was dead. The thought that there were men out there, an entire society trying to kill this woman, made his blood turn hot, inciting the primitive urge to wage war.

But he couldn't protect her forever. Once she met up with her colleague, she'd leave, and her safety would be out of his hands.

Troubled by that thought, he frowned. The path narrowed, and he took the lead. He rode in brooding silence as they skirted the ruins, then headed down the mountain through the mist. A rumble of thunder, the dull thud of their mounts' hoofbeats added to the somber mood.

He felt powerless, trapped. He couldn't have Dara; he had no doubts about that. But everything inside him rebelled at letting her go.

Minutes later, they rounded a boulder, and the gelding pricked his ears up and stopped. Alert now, Logan held out his arm to keep Dara behind him. "Someone's coming," he murmured. "Stay here."

He pulled out his rifle, worked a round into the chamber, urged Rupper farther ahead on the trail. The sniper might be dead, but Logan wasn't taking chances with Dara's life.

He stopped, waited. The thump of approaching hoofbeats reached his ears. One animal. Moving slowly.

A man came into view on the trail below. He rode a big sorrel mule, bigger than Logan's horse. The mule was heavily loaded, laboring beneath the weight of his rider and the bulging packs.

The rider glanced up, saw Logan aiming the weapon at him, and abruptly stopped. Their eyes met. The man's gaze flickered, but he didn't look away.

He was a tall man, light-complected, with a lanky build. He wore an Australian-style bush hat, a gun holster slung over his jacket. A camera dangled from his neck.

"Pedro?" Dara said. "What are you doing here?"

So this was the archeologist colleague. Logan waited another heartbeat until the man broke eye contact, then slowly lowered the gun. The colleague was younger than he had expected, about the same age he was.

"How did you get here?" Dara continued. She prodded her mule forward, rode up to Logan's side. "I was supposed to call you. How did you know where I was?"

Pedro flashed her a grin. "You won't believe it. It was sheer luck. We were renting mules, getting supplies when this old Quechua farmer came into town. There was an American medical group passing through, and they'd set up a mobile clinic across the plaza from where we were. The farmer stopped to talk to us on his way to see the doctors. It turns out he'd grown up in this area and knew where it was. I mean, what are the chances?"

Logan watched the interplay between the two, the way the colleague smiled at her, the too-familiar look in his eyes. Logan's face burned, his lips thinned. The thought goaded him, that Dara worked with this guy, laughed with him, spent hours in his company alone.

He clenched his jaw, realized that he was jealous. And he didn't like the feeling a bit.

Dara leaned forward in the saddle and glanced around. "So where's the team?"

"A few hours behind me. They were waiting for more supplies. I decided to ride ahead, see if you were still in the area. I couldn't wait to see the ruins." He shot her another smile, and Logan's gut seared even more.

Dara motioned toward him then, as if finally remembering he was here. "Pedro, this is Logan Burke, the man you told me to find."

The colleague met his gaze, inclined his head. "Good to meet you. I'm Dr. Hernandez."

Doctor Hernandez. Logan didn't miss the dig. The man was educated, spoke English fluently. Sharp intelligence gleamed in his eyes. Logan gave him a cold smile back.

Pedro shifted his attention to Dara. "So is Quillacocha far?"

"About half an hour up the trail."

Logan watched the exchange, reached a decision. There was no point going back to the ruins and hanging around with this man. It would only make him miserable, delay the inevitable. He'd promised to get Dara to her colleague, and he had.

She'd be safe now. He might not like the man, and he sure as hell didn't trust him. His instincts urged him to keep her in his sights. But the fierce jealousy roiling through him was skewing his judgment. Pedro was smart, armed, big. A team would join them soon. And the man who'd hunted her, the sniper, was dead.

Maybe it was better this way. He'd make a quick, clean break.

"Since you've found your colleague, I'll go now," he said. "It's shorter for me to turn back and head through the canyon."

Dara's gaze flew to his. Her lips parted. "You're leaving now?" She sounded shocked.

"I might as well. I'm not interested in the ruins. And your team's coming. They'll get you home."

"But…"

Pedro's eyes darted between them. "I'll wait ahead, take some photos of the mountains." He gestured to his camera, then kicked his mule, and rode off.

Logan kept his gaze on Dara. She stared back at him, her eyes stricken, her lower lip caught between her teeth. He gentled his voice. "It's better this way, darlin'."

"Right." Her mouth wobbled, and she blinked, averted her suddenly too-bright eyes.

He didn't know what to say. He rubbed the back of his neck, resettled his hat on his head. Hell. He didn't want to leave. In a perfect world, he'd stay with her, make love to her, spend the rest of his life in her arms. But he couldn't change reality or his past.

No matter how much he wished that he could.

He gazed at her for a long moment, memorizing the swell of her lips, the exotic tilt to her eyes, remembering her passion, her courage. His heart squeezed tight. A deep wrenching ache burned in his chest.

Unable to bear the agony, he wheeled the horse around and loped off. He reached a curve in the trail, hauled up on the reins and stopped, then braved a final glance back. She sat on the mule where he'd left her, watching him, looking so vulnerable, her eyes filled with such naked pain that it tore him apart. He ached to rush to her, comfort her, never let her go.

And then she lifted her chin, baring the elegant line of her throat, and pressed her lips into a smile. His regal princess.

His heart desolate, his entire world fracturing, he turned and rode away.

Dara plodded up the trail beside her colleague, her eyes wet with unshed tears, her stomach churned into shreds. She still couldn't believe that Logan had gone. She thought they'd have another day together, maybe two. But he'd ridden away. And now she would never see him again.

She dragged in a shuddering breath, feeling as if the mule had just kicked her chest. She wanted to curl up, huddle in a ball, block out the pain, the hurt.

Fortunately, Pedro didn't seem to notice her withdrawal. He chatted non-stop, his deep voice ringing with excitement as they rode back through the mist toward the ruins. He stopped to snap photos of the flora, the trail, marveled over every detail, turning ecstatic when he spotted a shrine. She'd never seen him so exuberant.

And she'd never felt so miserable. She inhaled around the

ache in her throat, blinked back a hot rush of tears. How could Logan have left her so abruptly? Didn't he care?

"Must be nearly sixteen thousand feet," Pedro exclaimed, and she forced herself to nod back. *Logan cared.* Even if he hadn't said it outright, she'd seen the tenderness in his eyes, felt the desire in his kiss.

But he didn't think he deserved her—which was ridiculous. She'd never met a more worthy man. He was noble, honorable, strong. Exactly the man she needed.

The man she loved.

She was tempted to turn the mule around, race after Logan, and beg him to let her stay. She'd gladly abdicate the throne. She'd never wanted to be a princess, and she would be thrilled to give it up.

But how could she abandon her people? Her conscience rebelled at the thought. They needed her. She was the only royal left. And they were in danger.

Logan's words echoed in her mind. *Fairy tales don't come true, Dara. Not even for a princess like you.*

He'd been right.

She let out an anguished sound.

Pedro glanced at her then. "That freight hauler, Logan Burke. Does he live near here?"

She nibbled her lip. Had Pedro noticed how depressed she was? She tried to stifle the quiver in her voice, to sound non-chalant. "I don't know. He never said." Logan hadn't shared much about his current life—where he stayed when he wasn't working, where he went.

"You were lucky to find him," Pedro said. "Quillacocha is an amazing discovery. The ruins alone…"

She tuned her colleague out, her heart aching so badly at the thought of Logan that it took all her effort not to bolt. But what was the point? She couldn't stay in Peru, and Logan wouldn't leave. And there was nothing she could say to change his mind. She'd told him she loved him. She'd asked him to come with her, and he'd said no. What else could she do?

They arrived at the crest of the hill above the ruins, and stopped the mules. For a long moment, neither spoke. She gazed down at the ruined city, the tendrils of fog snaking past the rocks. The mist had grown heavier, colder as the morning wore on, and she shivered in the gloomy chill. And a sudden, nervous feeling slunk through her nerves, like a premonition of evil, danger.

"Quillacocha," Pedro breathed, apparently oblivious to her dread. "Look at the size of it. It's huge! And there's the lake!"

She cast an uneasy glance at the moon-shaped lake. The waters seethed and roiled beneath the gunmetal clouds, turning a turbulent, tombstone gray. "Maybe we should hold off exploring it until the team gets here," she said.

"Are you nuts? This is the find of a lifetime. It's going to rock the world." His face flushed with excitement, Pedro lifted his camera, snapped off several shots.

Her gaze slid to the boulder where Logan had stood guard, then to the cliff where the sniper had died. She shivered, tried to block out the gruesome memories—the bloody altar, the sniper's horrified eyes as he fell.

The urge to bolt grew even more urgent, and she rubbed her arms, glanced back at the trail.

But Pedro leaped off his mule, still clutching his camera, and scrambled up a rock for a better view. "Look at this!" he raved. "There have to be mummies in those mountains."

Dara glanced toward the mausoleum where she'd found the dagger, watched the wisps of mist slither past. She shivered again, battled the sensation of impending doom.

Still grinning, Pedro jumped off the rock and strode back. "You haven't told me about the dagger. Where is it? I haven't even seen it yet."

She dismounted, strangely reluctant to show it to him. But that was silly. Pedro wasn't any danger to her. She was letting the gloom, her depression over Logan muddle her thoughts.

She unzipped her backpack, took out the dagger, unfolded the T-shirt she'd wrapped it in. The blade nearly vibrated in her hands, coursing with power, magic.

And her mind flashed back to Logan holding the dagger in the firelight, his big hand gripping the hilt, his biceps flexing as he slashed the air. He'd looked fierce, lethal, like a primitive Roma warrior. Her heart made a painful lurch.

She shook off the memory, tried to breathe through the growing anxiety. She walked to Pedro, held out the dagger. He reached for it with glittering eyes.

And a sudden spurt of fear jolted through her. She hesitated, struck by an awful sense of foreboding, telling her not to give the dagger to him, to run, to hide.

Logan's question whispered back—how well did she know her colleague? But this was Pedro. The man who'd helped her immensely over the years. She shook off the misgivings, handed him the blade.

"My God," he marveled. "I can feel the power in it. This is incredible." He let out a sharp, giddy laugh.

But a sick feeling pooled in her gut, making her nauseous, as if she'd done something wrong. She walked back to the mule to get some water, hoping to settle her nerves. But as she unlatched the pannier, Pedro's big sorrel mule shifted, bumping her with his heavy pack.

"Hey, watch out," she grumbled. She didn't need to get knocked off her feet.

She shoved the big mule with her shoulder, trying to push him out of the way, but a large, dark smear on the saddle blanket caught her eye.

A smear of dried blood.

Jittery now, she tilted her head. Was the mule injured? She lifted the edge of the blanket, but the hide beneath the spot looked fine.

Had Pedro been hurt then? The spot was near where his leg would rest when he sat in the saddle. She smoothed the blanket back into place, glanced at her colleague, but he was enthralled with the dagger, his eyes almost rabid with glee. He certainly didn't appear to be in pain.

Her gaze dipped to the ancient dagger in his hands, the grooved channels incised on the blade. Blood channels...

An image of the altar rose in her mind, the slaughtered llama's entrails, and her stomach made a queasy lurch. No way did she want to see that again. It had been bizarre, like a pagan sacrifice. Something the Inca would have done to appease the gods.

Pedro would be intrigued by it, though. He was an expert in Inca sacrificial rites...

Ice shimmered down her spine.

She jerked her gaze back to the blood on the blanket, and sudden chills beaded her skin. And a horrible thought wormed through her mind. What if Pedro hadn't come here with a team? What if he hadn't just arrived? What if he'd gotten to Quillacocha before they had and slaughtered that llama in an ancient rite?

But they'd found the llama on the trail that led up from the canyon.

The canyon where the farmers were killed.

Dara's hands froze on the pack, a metallic taste filling her mouth. Her mind flashed back to the altar, the symbol of the crescent moon.

Her entire body went cold.

A soft click shattered the silence. Unable to breathe, she slowly, slowly inched around.

And looked straight down the barrel of Pedro's gun.

His smile turned feral. "So, princess. You finally figured it out."

He'd done the right thing. He'd had to let her go. So why couldn't he convince himself of that?

Scowling, Logan loped through the gloomy canyon. Towering above him, the bloodred rocks glowered back. All down the trail, that damned restless feeling had tormented him, the feeling that something was wrong, that he shouldn't have left Dara with her colleague, that he'd made an awful mistake.

He exhaled through his teeth. The only mistake he'd made was letting himself get involved with her in the first place. She was safe. She was better off without him. Now he had to forget her, get on with his life, let her go.

The two mud huts came into view, and he eased Rupper into a walk. There was no reason to feel this jumpy. He'd been turning the details over in his head—the dead llama, the sniper's weapons, including the 9mm bullets he'd found in his pack—and there was no doubt the sniper was to blame. He'd ridden through this canyon, killed the farmers, then waited at the ruins to attack them.

Logan came to the farmers' grave, and stopped. The valley pulsed with an eerie silence. A sliver of fog drifted past. He loosened his grip on the reins, stared at the big stone he'd dragged over the grave.

He knew what was bothering him. He still didn't understand how the sniper had gotten around the landslide and arrived here so fast. But the man had been riding light, on a small, fast mule. And he might have known of a shortcut, even one of the secret passages the Inca had supposedly tunneled through the hills.

Logan leaped off the horse, left Rupper to graze in the grass as he quartered the area around the huts. He spotted the llama tracks, the mule tracks. He ducked into the hut where he'd found the man, the storage niches carved into the walls, scanned the clothes hanging from rough wooden pegs. Blood stained the dirt by the stools.

He fingered the 9mm casings he'd stuffed into his pocket, and that restless, uneasy feeling increased. He was missing something. Something important.

He strode from the hut, glanced around at the dreary mist, followed the mule tracks across the hard dirt. The woman had been shot in the freshly tilled section of earth enclosed by a low stone wall.

A sudden vision of Dara flitted through his mind—her face pained, her eyes vulnerable as he'd turned to go.

He pushed the fear aside. *She was safe.*

Just outside the stone wall, the earth turned soft, the mule tracks easier to see. He stopped, squatted on his heels, focused on the prints. They were clearly mule tracks, longer and narrower than those of a horse. The tracks were big, though, almost as big as his gelding's, and deep, sunk maybe three-quarters of an inch into the loose soil.

He narrowed his eyes, flashed back to Dara as he'd left her, sitting aside the sniper's mule. That mule was small, his packs light—too small, too light to make these tracks.

Which meant the sniper hadn't come this way. He'd gone up the main Inca trail, just as Logan had predicted. He'd still made good time, probably ridden through the nights while Logan and Dara slept. But he hadn't killed these farmers.

Someone riding a big, heavily laden mule had.

He closed his eyes, envisioned Dara's colleague on his sixteen-hand sorrel mule, the panniers bulging, the mule laboring under the weight.

"Oh hell."

His worst fear had just come true. He had left Dara to die.

Chapter 17

Dara gaped at the gun.

Pedro belonged to the secret society. Her trusted colleague. The man who'd mentored her for years.

And now he intended to kill her.

But she couldn't just stand here. She had to get away from him, fast!

Jolting herself into action, she dove between the mules. Pedro fired his gun, the noise deafening, and the two mules panicked and reared. She scrambled to get free, to get past their thrashing hooves, but they smashed into her, knocking her down as they stampeded away.

Her heart frenzied, she struggled to rise. But Pedro hurtled into her, slamming the breath from her lungs and flattening her to the ground. She cried out, twisted and bucked, but he was too heavy, too big to dislodge.

His knee dug into her spine. His heavy weight crushed her

chest. She wheezed, facedown, and panted for air, then kicked and writhed to get loose.

But he caught her arms, jerked them viciously behind her, and she gasped at the fierce streak of pain. She wriggled, kicked, tried desperately to knock him off.

But he shifted, pressed harder into her chest and throat, smothering the air from her lungs. Her head turned light. Her vision dimmed. She slumped against the dirt, unable to move as he bound her hands.

And then he rose, and she heaved in air. She wheezed, gagged, labored to haul oxygen through her burning throat. He'd nearly killed her. She blinked, fought off the waves of dizziness, rose awkwardly to her knees, barely able to maneuver with her hands tied.

Her lungs still searing, she glanced frantically around, tried to figure out how to escape. Her legs weren't tied. She could run...

The hard plastic barrel of the gun pressed her temple, and she stopped. Sweat beaded her skin. Terror reeked from her pores. Her world ground to a halt.

"I wouldn't try running," he said, and the wild excitement in his voice made her hair rise. "I don't need you anymore." He laughed then, a high-pitched sound that scared her even more.

He was right. He'd found Quillacocha. He had the dagger. She was as good as dead.

But she'd be damned if she'd act afraid. This was Pedro, her colleague. Who was he to shove her around?

He strolled around her, moved into her line of vision, and she forced up her chin. She was determined not to cower or let him see her fear. She ignored the pistol aimed at her skull, injected as much scorn into her voice as she could.

"A secret society, Pedro? Isn't that a bit *plebian* for your tastes? And please don't tell me you think you're the king?"

His face flushed, his eyes burned with hatred so intense that she flinched. Had she ever really known this man?

"I'm his tactician," he said, his voice fierce. "His right-hand man. And I'm more royal than you are, *princess*. My ancestors have been knights for a thousand years. You're nothing. A Gypsy! Thieves—that's all you people are. You stole what was rightfully ours."

"Tactician?" she scoffed back, forcing a bravado she didn't feel. "What have you ever planned?"

"I planned everything. I found the dagger, I came up with the plan to recover the necklace—it was all my work."

"*I* found the dagger," she argued. "And you weren't anywhere near that necklace. I was there at the ceremony, remember? I saw what happened that night."

His eyes chilled. He raised the gun, aimed it between her eyes. Panic mauled her throat.

"Of course I wasn't there. But I planned the heist. And my part went off flawlessly. We got the necklace, killed the Roma. If it hadn't been for that arrogant Spaniard…"

Dara's face turned hot. Fury scalded her veins. Pedro had planned her parents' murders? "Hardly flawless," she taunted. "Your man missed me."

"Dara, come on." His voice turned chiding, and he tilted his head. "Don't you understand? I had you spared. It was intentional. I knew you'd lead us to the dagger. You were already on the verge of finding it. I knew it wouldn't be long."

Dear God. He'd befriended her, worked with her because of the dagger.

"You had someone break into my apartment and kill my bodyguard," she said slowly.

He acknowledged that with a nod. "And when that failed, I had a man follow you here."

She stared at him, stunned that he could sound so indifferent. "Well, I have bad news for you, *Professor.* Your society's down by one. He's dead."

Pedro shrugged. "I would have killed him anyway. He wasn't one of us. He was a mercenary I hired to follow you and find the ruins. He was supposed to wait until he knew where the ruins were, then get rid of you, and bring me your notes. He didn't know about the dagger. I couldn't risk telling him in case he stole it for himself."

He made a sound of disgust. "But he was useless. I made it here without him. He didn't even get your notes."

She blinked, pieced together the events. So Pedro had arrived here first and looted the mausoleum. He'd probably searched for the sacred dagger, but hadn't discovered the hidden tomb. But it hadn't mattered. Like a fool, she'd handed the blade to him without a fight.

"And the llama? What was that about?"

He sighed, sounding disappointed, as if his prize student had failed a simple test. "The gods require sacrifices. You know that. And I was entering a holy site. Of course, I should have burned the flesh, but I couldn't risk the smoke."

He gave her a smile that curdled her blood. "But I'll make up for it. I'll do your sacrifice right. The gods prefer humans, you know. *Capacocha.* And you're perfect for it—beautiful, a virgin. Too old by Inca standards, but I think Villacocha will still approve."

He advanced on her then. She struggled to rise. An awful fear quaked in her throat.

"The Inca were humane," he continued, his voice oddly detached, as if he were lecturing his class. "The victims didn't suffer. The mummies we've recovered had their skulls crushed. This tells us that they were knocked unconscious before they were buried alive."

Terrified, she stumbled to her feet. She turned, tried to run, but Pedro was too fast. He grabbed her arm, jerked her back, slammed the gun into her head.

And then her world went black.

She awoke to brutal pain screaming through her skull. Intense spasms whipped through her head, the agony too piercing to bear. She whimpered, tried to escape back into oblivion, to make the horrendous pain disappear.

What had happened? Where was she? Her arms were numb. Her entire body felt battered, as if she'd been dragged over rocks. A dank smell permeated the air.

And then awareness rushed back—the dagger, Pedro! She stiffened, jerked open her eyes, reeled at the pain even that slight movement caused. She panted, struggled not to faint again, to clear the dark spots clouding her eyes.

The violent lashes eased, and she sucked in the fetid air. She was in a cave, she realized. *A tomb.* She was sitting on the floor, her body chilled from the frigid stones. Her arms were crossed over her breasts now, her legs bent in the fetal position. Pedro had tied ropes around her body so she couldn't move.

She squinted through the gloom, glanced at the empty niches carved into the walls. A sliver of light filtered through the darkness, prodding a memory, and she jerked her eyes to the side. A large, flat stone sat across the room, with a mummy curled up on top.

The blood drained from her head. Cold sweat popped from her pores. She was in the mummy's tomb. The tomb where she'd found the dagger. Pedro had left her here to die.

Panic swelled in her throat. She panted in quick, shallow gasps. He must have read the notes in her backpack and found the tomb. Or maybe she'd left footprints. She hadn't thought to cover her tracks.

And now the artifacts were gone from the niches, the gold plates stripped from the walls. Pedro must have worked for hours to loot the tomb.

And he'd been thorough. Nothing remained except the skeleton. Even the mummy's death mask was gone.

She stared at the bones curled in the fetal position, the dark sockets gaping in his skull.

Pedro had arranged her in exactly the same pose.

She choked back a frenzied scream.

Frantic, she glanced at the door, but the stone was firmly in place. She was tied up. She had no way out. Hysteria clouded her mind.

Calm down. *Calm down,* she urged herself fiercely. She desperately tried to think. Then she heard a scrape, a thud in the mausoleum chamber beyond the wall.

Pedro. He hadn't left yet.

"Pedro," she shouted. Pain ripped through her skull, and she gasped. But she couldn't worry about her head right now. This was her only chance to get free. "Pedro," she called again, trying to sound authoritative. "Get me out. You don't want to leave me here."

"You won't suffer," he called back, his voice muffled by the thick stone wall. "Villacocha will protect you."

Villacocha? The Inca creator god? Pedro actually believed that? Despair spiraled through her. Oh, God. He would never let her out. The man was nuts.

But then her anger sparked. Maybe she couldn't escape, but she wasn't going to let him ride blissfully off and lead a peaceful life. So he believed in ancient gods and superstitions? Well, then, she'd give him something to worry about at night.

"I curse you, Pedro Hernandez," she shouted. "In the name of my Roma ancestors. In the name of Sāti-Sara, the Gypsy goddess of fate. You will die. I swear to you, you will die. Pedro Hernandez, you are cursed!"

She inhaled, listened. Silence rocked in her ears.

And then a deep thud came from the outside chamber. Vibrations shook the ground. And she couldn't fight off the dread. Only one thing could have made that impact. He'd rolled the outer stone to the mausoleum in place.

She was trapped.

Her eyes locked on the mummy. Her hysteria rose. She was going to die here. Hundreds of years from now, she'd look like that mummy, her body decayed to bones.

A whimper escaped her. She lowered her head, buried her face in her knees, battled a surge of despair. And a vision of Logan came to mind—his rugged face, his determined stride. The thrilling way he'd looked at her with need in his hungry eyes. Tears burned behind her eyelids, blocking her throat, and she fought back the urge to weep.

But she couldn't cry, couldn't give up. Not yet. Not ever! She blinked back the tears, eyed the dim light shining through a crack overhead—light from a too distant source. Even if she could move, she'd never reach it.

Move. The command sliced through her brain. She bit down hard on her lip, ignored the sharp pain pummeling her skull, began scooting her way toward the door.

She couldn't let Pedro prevail, couldn't let that evil society win. She might not find a way out of this tomb; she might die here in the end.

But she was her people's leader. And she was going to try.

Logan leaped up the stone staircase three steps at a time, racing to get to the ruins. Why had he left Dara? Why had he ignored his instincts? His mistake might have gotten her killed.

No. She couldn't be dead. He couldn't fail, couldn't be too late again.

He reached the top of the stairs, his heart racing, and glanced around. The mist had grown heavier, blanketing the ruins in a ghostly fog. Nothing moved. Silence swelled. Moisture beaded and dripped off his hat.

He sprinted to the nearest boulder, flattened his back to the rock. He double-checked the pistol in his waistband, the ammunition in his pockets, the rifle's magazine. Then he inhaled, willed his pulse to calm, making himself focus, focus.

The dense mist swirled, and he tensed. The sniper's mule plodded into view.

Alone.

His gut went cold. Dara wouldn't have let the mule roam. Something must have happened to her.

His vision hazed, and a crazed, panicked feeling threatened his control, but he forced himself to think. Pedro must have taken her to the tombs. It was the only place to hide a corpse.

That thought broke through his composure, and he nearly went berserk. But he inhaled, exhaled, battled the urge to rush down there, to tear the ruins apart in a fit of rage. No matter how badly he wanted to find her, he had to stay calm. He couldn't afford to make a mistake.

His temples pounding, his jaw clamped so hard his molars ached, he peeked from behind the rock. The path was clear. He darted to the first ruined building and ducked inside.

He listened, waited a beat, rushed to the next room, and paused again. But the ruins were hushed, ominous. Too damned quiet.

Had Pedro already escaped? He suffered another spurt of dread. Pedro wouldn't leave unless Dara was dead.

Trying to block out that thought, to not let himself come undone, Logan worked his way through the ruins. But by the time he reached the low wall above the tombs, his control was nearly shot.

He crouched behind the wall, listened through the roar of his pulse. A mule stamped his hooves. Something metallic clanked. A man grumbled and swore.

The colleague. The man who intended to murder Dara.

Logan's blood surged. He bared his teeth and rose.

He spotted him mounting his mule. The mule's packs had been bulky before, but Pedro had tied big, gold plates over top and could barely squeeze into his seat.

Logan narrowed his eyes, raised his rifle, and aimed. But the mist shifted, obscuring the shot. He swore, leaped over the wall, ran through the fog toward the mule.

But Pedro glanced up and saw him. He wheeled the mule around. Logan raised his rifle and shot.

"No," Pedro screamed. "The curse can't work!" He urged the mule faster, spurring him toward the slope.

Logan sprinted behind him and scaled a rock, determined to get a clear shot. But the mule stumbled, the packs shifted, the gold plates rattled and banged.

Pedro panicked, tried to go faster. But the mule reared back, terrified by the noise, and the saddle slipped to the side.

Pedro lost his balance, began to fall. The mule bucked and tossed him off. He slammed into a rock and lay still.

His heart thundering, Logan raced to him. He kicked him over, kept his rifle pointed at his chest. But there was no need. His eyes were vacant. Logan lowered his gun, checked for a pulse. The man was dead.

He eyed the mule bucking up the slope. The packs broke loose, dropped to the ground, and the relieved mule trotted away.

Logan whirled, raced back to the tombs, urgency fueling his steps. Dara had to be in the mausoleum. Was she hurt? Unconscious? *Oh, hell. Don't let her be dead.*

"Dara," he shouted. He reached the mausoleum, eyed the big stone door. He tossed down his rifle, sprinted over.

And spotted the bundle of explosives strapped to one side.

His heart stopped. Fear coiled deep in his chest. Pedro had rigged the caves to blow.

With Dara inside.

He rushed to inspect the dynamite charge. Pedro had banded half a dozen sticks together, taped on a timer. Logan glanced at the clock, and his heart went wild.

There were only three minutes left.

He couldn't disarm it. He didn't have time. He might choose the wrong wires, blow himself up instead.

He had to get Dara out fast.

He lunged for the stone that sealed the mausoleum, braced his shoulder against it, and shoved. Sweat streamed down his jaw, and he heaved again.

The rock inched aside. He grunted, shoved harder, wedged open a space wide enough to slip through. He squeezed into the cave, glanced around, but it was empty. *Damn!*

"Dara," he called again.

"I'm here," she answered, and relief spurted through him. "In the mummy's tomb. Behind the wall."

Frantic now, knowing time was running out, he raced to the wall where he'd heard her voice. How many seconds were left?

"Where's the door?" he shouted.

"Near the floor. To the right. There's a symbol on it, a moon."

He scanned the floor, saw a space where the dust had been disturbed. He rushed to the stone, gripped the edge, and pulled. It didn't budge, and his desperation surged. "Can you push it?"

"I'll…try. But my feet are tied."

He yanked harder. Nothing happened. He jerked and pulled again.

"I'm pushing," she cried.

The stone rocked loose. He grabbed the edge, hurled it from the space, then wriggled through the low opening. He spotted Dara beside him, all bound up.

And then the dynamite blew.

Chapter 18

Logan was here.

Dara lay plastered beneath him as the explosion ripped through the cave. Her skull throbbed at the horrendous racket. Vibrations rattled her jaw. Logan crushed her into the floor, his big body sheltering hers, while rocks shuddered and crashed all around.

A stone thudded close by, and she flinched, prayed that they wouldn't get hit. The earth trembled and groaned from the impact. Falling dirt choked the air. And then finally, miraculously, the deafening blast receded. The ground stopped shaking. Her heartbeat began to slow.

Logan lifted himself away, and she gasped in a lungful of dust. She coughed, moaned, as more pain sliced through her head. She rolled onto her back and jerked her gaze to Logan. His hat was gone, dirt coated his shoulders and hair. And he looked so rugged, so wonderful, so heroic that her eyes burned, her throat turned thick with tears. She ached to hurl herself into his arms.

But she was still tied up.

"Are you all right?" He lunged toward her, grabbed her arms, helped her sit up. His gaze roved her face, her legs.

"Yes, I—" She coughed again, winced at the pain wracking her skull. "Oh, God…"

"Here." He whipped his knife from his boot, sawed at the ropes binding her chest. The ropes broke free, and fierce needles shot through her limbs.

"Don't move," he warned. "Let the circulation come back first." He crowded close, rubbed her arms, her hands, her legs. And she just sat there, shredded inside, inhaling his wonderful warmth, longing to curl into him and weep.

She'd almost died. But Logan had saved her. A huge lump constricted her throat.

He ran his hands over her shoulders, her back, then cradled her jaw. His gaze met hers. And she saw emotions parade through her eyes—fear, urgency. Love?

Her breath caught. Hot tears blurred her eyes. And then he dipped his head to hers and kissed her, his lips comforting, safe, and she sobbed against his mouth, at the joy of him, the thrill of him, overcome by gratitude and relief.

His kiss eased, and he pulled back. He rested his forehead against hers, and his warm breath fanned her lips. His hand slid to her throat, threaded her hair. She winced at the swift jab of pain.

He jerked back, his eyes filled with concern. "What is it? What happened?"

"My head. It's…Pedro. He knocked me out."

"Let me see." She bent her head, and his big hands sifted gently through her hair. And then he stopped, hissed. "Good thing he's dead or I'd kill him for this."

Her heart skipped. She lifted her head and met his gaze. "He's dead?"

"Yeah." His eyes turned dark. His hand slid to her jaw, and his big thumb stroked her throat. "I'll tell you about it later. Let's get out of here first."

She nodded, shaken by the news. Had her curse...? No, that was ridiculous. But she shivered, realized she didn't want to know how Pedro had died. At least not yet.

Logan rose, tugged her to her feet. She waited a second for the trembling to pass, then turned her attention to the tomb.

Several rocks had fallen from the ceiling, turning the crack of light into a gaping hole. But the rest of the tomb was surprisingly intact. "These ruins have withstood earthquakes," she said.

Logan poked his head through the doorway, scooted back in. "Maybe so, but the outer chamber didn't make it. It took the brunt of the blast. It's blocked."

"We can't get through?"

He shook his head, dislodging dust. "Maybe eventually. But it would take days."

Days. She swallowed, glanced around. There were no other entrances into this tomb. Her gaze returned to the open space above.

"I'll see if I can climb up there," he said, obviously coming to the same conclusion. He strode to a big rock that had fallen near the mummy, and paused.

"This is where I found the dagger," she said, and then her breath caught. "I gave it to Pedro."

"We'll find it." He squatted, muscled the rock across the room. "His packs are outside the cave."

"Thank goodness." She'd hate to think this had all been in vain. But they still weren't out of danger. They had to get out of the tomb.

Logan positioned the stone beneath the hole, climbed on top. He stretched, gripped the sides of the opening, then hoisted himself up. His biceps bulged. His shoulders flexed. The veins stood out in his arms.

And Dara could only stare. She'd never seen a stronger, more sinfully attractive man. He braced his forearms in the opening, swung his muscled legs through the hole.

"We can get out this way," he called down, and relief flooded through her. He poked his head back through the hole. "But it's steep."

Steep. Oh, God. Not more heights.

But what choice did she have?

Pushing aside her fear, she scrabbled onto the rock. Logan reached down, and she grabbed his hands. His warm, callused hands. Their eyes locked, and her love for him swelled.

"Hold on, darlin'," He pulled her up, dragged her through the opening onto a rock. "Careful now," he said. He held her arm as she sprawled beside him. She blinked in the gloomy daylight, sucked in the cool, moist air. And then she glanced down.

And froze.

They'd come out on a slanted ledge, barely two feet wide, near the top of a sheer granite cliff.

A cliff that plunged a thousand feet to the river below.

She pressed herself flat against the rock and closed her eyes.

"You can do this," Logan said. "We've only got twenty feet to go."

She opened her eyes, struggled to breathe, but her entire body started to shake. They had to walk twenty feet across a sloping rock slick with mist. One tiny slip…

"I'll go first," he added. "You can hold on to my shirt."

As if he could keep her from falling. She would pull him with her if she slipped. A whimper rose in her throat.

She swallowed, nearly swooned. This was every nightmare she'd ever had.

But she knew she had to move. The longer she sat here, the more terrified she'd become.

Her heart thudding, her legs wobbling so hard her kneecaps

jumped, she slowly, slowly rose to her feet. She panted, tried to ignore the dizziness lashing her head, locked her jaw to still her wildly clacking teeth.

Breathe, she told herself fiercely. Keep your eyes on Logan. *Don't look down.*

"All right. Let's get off this rock."

She grabbed the end of his T-shirt. He started to move and her panic surged. "Wait!" she gasped, and he stopped.

She inhaled through her clenched teeth, beat back the hysteria swarming her chest. "Okay. Okay."

He nodded, stepped forward again, and she forced her feet to move. Time stalled. A terrible nausea rose. She kept her eyes glued to Logan's back as she minced across the ledge, inch by excruciating inch, breathing, breathing.

And then suddenly, Logan grabbed her hand and leaped the final distance, jerking her from the rock. She fell through the air, collapsed against him on solid ground, so relieved she started to cry. They'd made it. They were finally, finally safe.

Still beneath her, Logan wrapped his arms around her back. And tears streaked her cheeks, blocked up her throat. She gripped his shoulders, ran her hands over his face, his cheeks.

And he cupped her chin, splayed his hand across her neck. His dark eyes burned into hers. "I'm sorry," he said, his voice rough. "I'm so damned sorry I almost failed you."

"It wasn't your fault," she whispered back, her own voice raw with tears. "I should have realized it was him when you found the llama."

He pulled her head down and kissed her then, sliding his mouth over hers. It was a kiss of desperation, need. Hunger and want. And she moaned, thrilling to his lips, his scent, the rough feel of the man she loved. She never wanted to let him go.

But he broke away, pressed her head to his chest. His uneven breath feathered her ear. He was her hero. Her destined mate.

The man she wanted to spend eternity with. She could never bear it if he left her now.

"Come with me," she pleaded. "Please come back with me. I love you, Logan. And I need you so much."

He didn't answer, and she lifted her head. She saw the pain, the denial clouding his eyes. "Hell, Dara. Don't you know how much I'd like that?"

"But then—"

"I can't," he said, his voice strained. "Nothing's changed."

"But how can you say that? You saved me. How much proof do you need?"

He shook his head, rolled from beneath her, and rose, and she stared up at him, incredulous that he still didn't see the truth. "Logan... You made a mistake once. You're allowed to. You're human. Nobody's perfect. You don't have to punish yourself forever. You're allowed some happiness in your life."

He exhaled, gripped the back of his neck, and looked away. And she knew that she was losing him. Her desperation rose. "I can't believe you're doing this." Ignoring the pain thrashing her skull, she leaped to her feet. Frustration tightened her voice. "I need you. We're perfect for each other. You know we are. And all you're doing is running away. You're using the past as an excuse not to get involved."

He walked back to her then, stepped close, lifted her chin. And in his eyes she saw pain, regret, love. He loved her. She felt it as clearly as if he'd shouted it out. "I'm going to miss you like hell," he rasped.

And then he stepped back. Her chest tightened, her eyes burned, and a huge surge of despair swarmed her throat. But she knew that no matter what she said, no matter what she did, she wouldn't change his mind.

Their journey was done.

* * *

The downpour hammered the tin roof of the village bar. The racket drummed through Logan's temples, drowning out his thoughts, which was fine with him. He didn't want to think, didn't want to feel.

He braced his arm on the bar, shifted his weight to ease the damp cold seeping through his boots, and tossed back his second shot of whiskey. It scorched through his belly, briefly banishing the chill that had settled in his bones.

But not the loneliness.

Exactly one month had passed since Dara had left Peru. Thirty-one days. Seven hundred, forty-four hours. And he'd ached for her every minute, every second of every day.

He scowled, fingered his empty shot glass, signaled the bartender for another round. He knew it wouldn't do any good. No amount of alcohol, no discomfort, no matter how severe, could ease the pain in his heart.

God knew he'd tried. He'd spent the past month driving himself to exhaustion, riding Rupper over the steepest terrain in freezing rain and sleet. He'd finally had to stop before he killed his horse.

He shifted his gaze to the open doorway, watched the blowing sheets of rain strafe the mud. And he had to admit he had no desire to head out there, no desire to hike over yet another mountain alone. This seclusion, this exile in the wilderness didn't appeal to him anymore.

He missed Dara too much.

Lightning crackled. Thunder rumbled under his boots. He downed the shot of whiskey, eyed the small family huddled by the door. They'd ducked into the bar, waiting for the worst of the storm to pass.

His gaze skimmed the woman, a typical villager with her layered sweaters and skirts, her dusty bowler hat. She had a baby slung over her back in a colorful blanket, sandals on her dark, bony feet. Next to her stood a young boy, maybe eleven, twelve years old, skinny and tall, with that gawky, pre-teen frame.

The woman looked too old, the kid too innocent and young. But Logan hadn't been much older than that when his mother had died.

When he'd headed into the mines.

Dara's words echoed in his mind, he sighed. He'd thought about the past since she'd left, and he knew that she was right. He wasn't responsible for his mother's death. He'd done his best to help her, but he had been a child.

But his wife. He shook his head. No matter how he examined that situation, he had to accept the blame. True, they'd had a bad marriage. They never should have married; they hadn't been suited at all. Now that he'd met Dara, he could clearly see the difference.

And if María had lived, they would have divorced. That trip had been a last-ditch effort to save a marriage that had already reached its end.

María had been spoiled, hot-tempered, impulsive. He couldn't have stopped her from riding off. But he had waited too long, given her too much of a lead, before he'd gone in pursuit. He had expected her to cool off and come back.

He'd miscalculated, made a mistake—a bad one. One he would always regret.

But was Dara right? Should he forgive himself for not being perfect? Had he paid for that mistake long enough?

He fished some coins from his pocket, dropped them onto the bar, unable to block out the rest of her words. Was he running away? Was he using his guilt as an excuse to avoid getting involved?

Was he a coward?

His gut stilled. He tightened his jaw, scowled up at the

noisy tin roof, wishing the rain had drummed out that thought, because he sure as hell didn't like it.

But he couldn't avoid the truth anymore. She was right. He was running away, hiding out in the hills because he was afraid to make another mistake.

So like a fool, he'd let her go. He'd let the only woman he'd ever loved leave.

And made the biggest mistake of all.

She missed Peru.

Dara sat at her computer in her seaside apartment, her elbows propped by the keyboard, her chin cradled in her hands, staring at the Machu Picchu screen saver on the monitor. She gazed at the rugged peaks, the plunging, terraced slopes, the mist hovering over the Urubamba River rushing hundreds of feet below.

She scrubbed her face in her hands, flopped back in her chair and groaned. Who was she fooling? It wasn't Peru she missed. It was Logan.

She missed everything about that man—his face, his voice, his seductive, masculine scent. Day after day she kept thinking of things to tell him, questions she wanted to ask him, details of her life she wanted to share.

And the nights... The nights were pure misery. She ached for him, burned for him. She kept reliving his kiss, the breath-taking way he'd touched her, the shattering pleasure she'd found in his arms.

Disgusted with herself, she shoved her chair from the desk and rose, then threaded her way through the piles of packed boxes to the window overlooking the beach. A winter storm had moved in overnight, turning the sky a sheet-metal gray. High surf pounded and dragged at the sand. A piece of driftwood bobbed in the frothy whitewater, dithering endlessly back and forth between the shore and open sea.

She felt just as adrift, just as torn. For the moment, she was back in her own apartment, trying to get used to the increased police protection and bodyguards her uncle had arranged. Nicu had taken over her security detail, carefully screening her visitors, insisting she didn't leave home without at least two guards.

Thankfully, the media furor had finally died down. For the first few weeks, she couldn't leave her apartment without being mobbed. Everyone wanted to hear about the dagger, the lost Inca city, Pedro's horrific death. The frenzy had eased once the dagger was put under international protection with the necklace, and safely stored away.

But she still felt edgy, rootless. And she couldn't quell the terrible dread, that unceasing ball of misery, the realization that Logan was gone. She'd done everything she could to forget him. She'd resigned from her position at the university. She'd thrown herself into her duties as princess and searched for a different job.

But when she'd found herself applying for a research position in Texas, she'd finally faced the truth. She was hopeless. Pathetic. She was willing to move a thousand miles just to hear a sexy drawl.

A knock on the door interrupted her thoughts. "Come in," she called, relieved to have even a momentary diversion from her thoughts about the man she loved.

The door opened, and her uncle Nicu popped his balding head inside. "Have you got a minute?"

"Sure." Anything was better than staring at her Machu Picchu screen saver while she pretended not to think about Logan. "What's up?"

Nicu stepped into the room and closed the door. His gaze flicked to the armchairs arranged around a coffee table in the corner, then back to her. "Mind if I sit down?"

She blinked. "That sounds serious." Nicu rarely lingered to

chat. He was the busiest man she knew, a confirmed workaholic dedicated to the Roma cause. "Don't tell me I'm in trouble."

His smile was tight. "No, but I might be."

Her stomach dipped. "Something's really wrong?" His steps were slow as he crossed the room, as if he were dreading the conversation ahead, and her own nerves tensed. "You're scaring me, Nicu. What is it?"

He perched his bulky frame on the edge of a seat, clasped his hands over his knees. When he didn't speak, the flutter in her belly grew. What could be that hard to say?

He palmed his balding forehead, let out a heavy sigh. "There's something I need to tell you. Something I should have said long ago." He glanced away again, and her pulse pattered hard. Worried now, she rose, and took a seat on the opposite chair.

"I promised your father I'd tell you this if anything happened to him." His eyes met hers, skittered away, and she felt a spurt of dread.

"Tell me what?" If this was bad news, she wasn't sure she wanted to hear.

He sighed. "I told you why we left Romanistan, right?"

She frowned, confused. Why bring that old history up? "There was a coup."

"Right. The year you were born there was a lot of turmoil. There were attacks on the palace, bombs, assassination attempts. Spies everywhere. We didn't know who we could trust."

"So?" None of this seemed important now.

"So your mother went into labor at the worst possible time. And she had a hard delivery. She needed an emergency C-section. The doctor…" He clasped his hands. "We were worried, Dara. We all thought she would die. And then a bomb went off, throwing everything in chaos.

"We heard that assassins had infiltrated the palace. Your

father was frantic. He thought we'd all be killed. And your mother was too ill to move." His eyes met hers. "We did what we thought was best—best for the family, for Romanistan. Believe me, we never meant to do any harm."

She frowned. "Go on."

Nicu exhaled. "He asked me to take the baby to a convent. Just for a while, to keep her safe. Just until things calmed down and it was safe to bring her back."

Bring *her* back? The fluttering in her belly grew.

Nicu shot her a pleading look. "The plan backfired. The convent was attacked. Most of the nuns died—and the baby disappeared. I searched. Believe me, I searched. And your father…" He shook his head, closed his eyes. "I thought he would rip the city apart. I've never seen a more desperate man."

Dara's heart rolled. A dull roar battered her skull. She parted her lips, but couldn't speak.

"Your mother was ill for days," Nicu continued. "We were sure she wouldn't survive. We couldn't bear to tell her the truth."

The truth. Nicu's gaze met hers. And she saw the sorrow in his eyes, the pain. And suddenly, she knew. "You mean…"

He nodded. "We brought in an orphan. Your mother hadn't seen the baby yet, and we thought if she died… At least she'd die happy. At least she'd think her daughter had lived."

The walls of the room pressed down. Dara forced in a shallow breath. And everything she knew about herself turned into a lie.

"You're that orphan," her uncle confirmed. "You aren't the real princess."

Chapter 19

She wasn't the princess.

Then who on earth was she?

Dara stared at her uncle Nicu, her whole world cracking apart. But if what Nicu said was true, then he wasn't her uncle. Her world tilted even more.

She shook her head, feeling lost, disoriented, unable to process it all. This couldn't be real, could it?

"I…" She scrambled for something to say. But what could she say? It was too unbelievable, too shocking.

"We were sure the princess was dead," Nicu continued. "And when the queen started to recover…" He lifted his hand. "She couldn't have more children. And we thought, well, it would have been too cruel to tell her then that her daughter was dead. We thought it was better to just let it go, to not let the secret out."

"To let me be the princess?" Her voice sounded too far away.

"It wasn't only because of her." He sighed again, more heavily this time. "There were political motives, too. The people needed hope. They needed to believe that the royal line would go on. And if the real princess was alive by some miracle, we knew she'd be in danger. We couldn't let out the truth until we could keep her safe."

"I see," Dara said, still stunned, still grappling to make sense of it all. But this was so incredible, so bizarre.

"I wanted to tell you before this," Nicu added, and his eyes met hers. "The guilt weighed on me. I thought I was doing the right thing back then. I really did. But now... I'm not so sure. Maybe it wasn't fair to you."

"But my mother—"

"She never knew. We wanted to tell her, but the more time went on..." He spread his hands. "I promised your father I'd tell you the truth if anything happened to him. But after he died, we were busy with the funeral, and then you went into protective custody."

And then she'd run off to Peru.

"I understand, I think." But what should she do with this news? She tugged on her lip, tried to wrap her mind around this amazing twist.

She wasn't the princess. It was incredible. But it also explained so much. Why she'd been so different from her parents. Why she'd found it hard to conform.

Her mother had found her frustrating, perplexing. They'd knocked heads all her life. But her father... He'd been gentle with her, patient. Maybe to compensate?

Her father's face flashed into her mind with sudden clarity, and she pictured his familiar brown eyes, that expression of regret. But maybe she'd misinterpreted that look all these years. She frowned. "My father—"

"He loved you, Dara. He never cared that you weren't his by blood. He was just sorry he'd dragged you into this."

She swallowed. All those years. It had killed her to see him looking at her like that, with disappointment—or so she'd thought. She'd wanted so desperately to please him, to measure up. Even her search for the dagger had been an attempt to prove her worth.

She met her uncle's eyes. "You have no idea who I am then?"

"No. The hospital records were destroyed in the bombings. There's no way to know who your real parents were."

Her real parents. She blinked at that odd thought. She might have brothers, sisters... And then more implications rushed in. If she wasn't the princess, she was free. Free to go back to Peru. Free to live the life she wanted.

Free to be with Logan, the man she loved.

She jumped up, restless suddenly, and crossed to the window. Her excitement growing, she gazed out at the stormy beach. She could leave this life behind, hunt Incan artifacts to her heart's content.

An old woman hobbled to the edge of the beach just then, catching Dara's eye. Her loose pants flapped, her shoulders hunched against the breeze as she trundled across the soft sand. The woman looked lonely on the empty beach, fragile.

Like her people. Dara's heart plunged. *Her people.* What could she do about them? She couldn't leave them without a leader. They'd have no one to speak for them, fight for them. They'd be devastated if she abandoned them now.

And it would embolden the enemy. The Order of the Black Crescent Moon would be thrilled to have her gone. There would be more killings, more innocent people dead.

It would be worse than that. If the real princess was alive, she probably didn't know who she was. She didn't even know that she was in danger. And if word leaked out, if the evil society found her before the Roma did, they'd never let her survive.

Which meant that Dara was trapped. She couldn't change her life, couldn't let anyone know she wasn't the princess—not until they found the real heiress to the throne.

If they found her. Her uncle doubted she was even alive.

Dara turned. "You really think she's dead?"

His eyes filled with regret. "We looked everywhere, Dara. We had to do it secretly, but believe me, we searched. We couldn't even find the medallion."

She furrowed her brows. "What medallion?"

"When I took her to the convent, I tucked a good-luck charm into her blankets. Maybe it was superstitious, but I figured it couldn't hurt. And it could help us identify her later on. But it vanished with her."

He shot her an apologetic look. "I'm sorry, Dara. Your father would have told you sooner, but he didn't want to cause your mother pain. And he said to tell you—if this moment came—to let your heart guide you. To do what you think is best. He said you'd know what to do."

Dara rubbed her forehead. It was all so complicated. She'd have to rethink everything now—her father's guilt, her identity. But Nicu was right. She had to decide what to do.

"We have to search again," she said, sure of that much. "We have to make every attempt to find the real princess. But we need to keep it a secret. If word gets out, and the Black Crescent Society find her before we do, they'll kill her. And she won't even know she's in danger. She won't know to protect herself."

He nodded. "I'll start the search right away." His eyes met hers, filled with concern. "But Dara, I just want you to know, no matter what happens…"

"I know." A sudden ease slid through her heart. "I'm okay with this, Nicu. I really am. Whatever happens, I'll be fine."

He smiled back, a warm smile that gentled his eyes. "I know your mother was hard on you, but she really did love you. You kept her alive, you know. And now… She'd be proud of you, Dara. She'd say you make the perfect queen." He rose and left the room.

Dara's throat closed. Tears burned behind her eyes. That was the nicest thing he'd ever said. After a lifetime of disappointing her mother, of never fitting in or acting right, he'd said that she would be proud.

But the terrible irony didn't escape her. If she wasn't the princess, then her wildest dream had just come true. And yet, it changed nothing. She had to continue the charade until they found the real princess—maybe forever if the other woman wasn't alive.

She closed her eyes, thought of Logan, and a terrible desolation swelled in her chest. Logan, the one man who understood her, who accepted her. The man she desperately loved.

The man she could never have. Because no matter how much she ached to follow her heart, she couldn't abandon her people. Logan had taught her that. He'd shown her the meaning of honor. He'd sacrificed his needs to do the right thing.

Now for honor's sake, she had to be the princess her people deserved. Even if she had to forfeit her heart.

Logan stood in the hallway of Dara's beachside apartment, his arms crossed, so tense he could hardly breathe. What if she didn't forgive him? What if she'd changed her mind since she'd returned? What the hell would he do?

He glanced at the uniformed guards eyeing him from down the hall, then at Dara's uncle by his side. The older man had welcomed him, thanked him for protecting Dara, seemed genuinely glad he was here.

But would Dara? He cleared his suddenly parched throat.

The uncle raised his hand to the door and knocked. The sharp rap drummed through his nerves.

"Come in," Dara called, and his heart sped up.

Her uncle pushed open the door. "You have a visitor." He motioned Logan inside, gave him an encouraging smile, and closed the door.

Grateful that the uncle had given them privacy, Logan paused, glanced around the chaotic room. There were boxes on the desk, beside the chairs, stacked three-high along the walls. His gaze narrowed in on Dara near the desk, bending over a box as she taped it closed.

His heart thudded to a stop. The air felt kicked from his lungs. And like an addict in the throes of withdrawal, he devoured every inch of her—the curve of her back, the flare of her hips. Her hair was loose, and the long, shiny mass swung over her shoulder, hiding her face from view. She straightened, pushed the hair from her eyes, and turned.

Her gaze collided with his. Her lips parted, and she froze.

His stomach balled. His heartbeat accelerated, and his gaze hungrily swept over her—those witchy eyes, her pouting lips, the full, high swell of her breasts.

She was beautiful. Mesmerizing. Brave. Everything he'd ever wanted. Far more than he deserved.

How had he let her go?

He swallowed around the dust clogging his throat, forced his vocal chords to work. "I've been a fool, Dara." His voice came out rusty and deep.

She didn't move. She just stared at him as if paralyzed. The uncertainty tore at his gut.

And then her soft lips trembled. Her eyes misted with tears.

And he couldn't stand it anymore. He strode across the room, leaped over a box, hauled her roughly into his arms—and did what he'd been aching to do for weeks. He slanted his mouth over hers, plundered her lips, her mouth, ravishing her, venting his hunger, his yearning, his need.

He fisted her hair with his hand, growled deep in his throat, lost in the torrid kiss. He knew he was too rough, too desperate, but he couldn't temper the staggering need. He jerked her tightly against him, pulling her curves to his rock-hard frame. And he kissed her deeper, harder, inhaling her seductive scent, while his hunger surged out of control.

But then a glimmer of sanity returned, breaking through the delirium, and he managed to lift his head. And he brushed her jaw with his thumb, gazed into her glistening eyes—at the woman who'd healed him, who'd brought him out of his solitude, back into the land of the living, the light.

The woman who made him complete.

"I love you," he said. "Will you forgive me, marry me? I'll stay here," he added when her eyes brimmed with tears. "I'll do whatever you need me to do. I'm just too damned lonely without you."

Her lips wobbled, and tears slid down her cheeks. He wiped away a drop with his thumb. His chest swelled tight, his lungs ached. "Will you?" he asked again, unable to stand the suspense.

"Yes." Her voice trembled, and she cleared her throat. "*Yes, of course, I will.*" Her lips curved into a smile, a warm, wondrous smile that lit his soul.

Still holding her close, unable to let her go, he tugged a ring from the pocket of his jeans. "We can buy a different ring," he said, suddenly nervous. "This gold…the miners…"

"It's perfect," she whispered, her eyes shining. "You're perfect. Oh, Logan. I love you so much."

His throat thick, his hands shaking, he slid the ring on her slender finger, then folded his hand over hers. And he gazed into her soft, warm eyes, hardly able to believe his luck, that this woman would forever be his.

But she reached up with her other hand, pulled his head down to hers, fusing their lips in a deep, searing kiss that didn't leave any doubt.

"How soon can we get married?" he rasped when they finally broke apart.

"Right now?" Her voice was breathless. "We could elope."

"Can a princess do that?"

She laughed. "That's just it. You'll never believe it, but it turns out I'm not the princess."

He listened as she told him about her uncle's revelation, but the feel of her clouded his mind. He nuzzled her neck, her jaw, while his hands roamed from her back to her hips.

Her breath grew ragged. Her eyes looked blurred. And when he succumbed to temptation and stroked her breasts with his thumbs, she moaned.

"But I have to stay the princess for now," she added in a strangled voice. "Until we find her. If we find her. It's too dangerous to let anyone know."

His heart swelled. She was amazing. She was willing to forfeit her needs for the people, willing to serve as a decoy and risk her life until the real princess was found.

But the real miracle was that she'd fallen in love with him.

"Real or not, you'll always be a princess to me." And no matter where her duties took her, no matter how long she had to live the royal life, he would stay by her side.

Because she'd given him love, the greatest treasure of all.

* * * * *

Here is a sneak preview of
A STONE CREEK CHRISTMAS,
the latest in Linda Lael Miller's acclaimed
MᴄKETTRICK *series.*

A lonely horse brought vet Olivia O'Ballivan to Tanner
Quinn's farm, but it's the rancher's love that might cause
her to stay.

A STONE CREEK CHRISTMAS
Available December 2008
from Silhouette Special Edition.

Tanner heard the rig roll in around sunset. Smiling, he wandered to the window. Watched as Olivia O'Ballivan climbed out of her Suburban, flung one defiant glance toward the house and started for the barn, the golden retriever trotting along behind her.

Taking his coat and hat down from the peg next to the back door, he put them on and went outside. He was used to being alone, even liked it, but keeping company with Doc O'Ballivan, bristly though she sometimes was, would provide a welcome diversion.

He gave her time to reach the horse Butterpie's stall, then walked into the barn.

The golden retriever came to greet him, all wagging tail and melting brown eyes, and he bent to stroke her soft, sturdy back. "Hey, there, dog," he said.

Sure enough, Olivia was in the stall, brushing Butterpie down and talking to her in a soft, soothing voice that touched something private inside Tanner and made him want to turn on one heel and beat it back to the house.

He'd be damned if he'd do it, though.

This was *his* ranch, *his* barn. Well-intentioned as she was, *Olivia* was the trespasser here, not him.

"She's still very upset," Olivia told him, without turning to look at him or slowing down with the brush.

Shiloh, always an easy horse to get along with, stood contentedly in his own stall, munching away on the feed Tanner had given him earlier. Butterpie, he noted, hadn't touched her supper as far as he could tell.

"Do you know anything at all about horses, Mr. Quinn?" Olivia asked.

He leaned against the stall door, the way he had the day before, and grinned. He'd practically been raised on horseback; he and Tessa had grown up on their grandmother's farm in the Texas hill country, after their folks divorced and went their separate ways, both of them too busy to bother with a couple of kids. "A few things," he said. "And I mean to call you Olivia, so you might as well return the favor and address me by my first name."

He watched as she took that in, dealt with it, decided on an approach. He'd have to wait and see what that turned out to be, but he didn't mind. It was a pleasure just watching Olivia O'Ballivan grooming a horse.

"All right, *Tanner*," she said. "This barn is a disgrace. When are you going to have the roof fixed? If it snows again, the hay will get wet and probably mold..."

He chuckled, shifted a little. He'd have a crew out there the following Monday morning to replace the roof and shore up the walls—he'd made the arrangements over a week before—but he felt no particular compunction to explain that. He was enjoying her ire too much; it made her color rise and her hair fly when she turned her head, and the faster breathing made her perfect breasts go up and down in an enticing rhythm. "What makes you so sure I'm a greenhorn?" he asked mildly, still leaning on the gate.

At last she looked straight at him, but she didn't move from Butterpie's side. "Your hat, your boots—that fancy red truck you drive. I'll bet it's customized."

Tanner grinned. Adjusted his hat. "Are you telling me real cowboys don't drive red trucks?"

"There are lots of trucks around here," she said. "Some of them are red, and some of them are new. And *all* of them are splattered with mud or manure or both."

"Maybe I ought to put in a car wash, then," he teased. "Sounds like there's a market for one. Might be a good investment."

She softened, though not significantly, and spared him a cautious half smile, full of questions she probably wouldn't ask. "There's a good car wash in Indian Rock," she informed him. "People go there. It's only forty miles."

"Oh," he said with just a hint of mockery. "*Only* forty miles. Well, then. Guess I'd better dirty up my truck if I want to be taken seriously in these here parts. Scuff up my boots a bit, too, and maybe stomp on my hat a couple of times."

Her cheeks went a fetching shade of pink. "You are twisting what I said," she told him, brushing Butterpie again, her touch gentle but sure. "I meant…"

Tanner envied that little horse. Wished he had a furry hide, so he'd need brushing, too.

"You *meant* that I'm not a real cowboy," he said. "And you could be right. I've spent a lot of time on construction sites over the last few years, or in meetings where a hat and boots wouldn't be appropriate. Instead of digging out my old gear, once I decided to take this job, I just bought new."

"I bet you don't even *have* any old gear," she challenged, but she was smiling, albeit cautiously, as though she might withdraw into a disapproving frown at any second.

He took off his hat, extended it to her. "Here," he teased. "Rub that around in the muck until it suits you."

She laughed, and the sound—well, it caused a powerful and wholly unexpected shift inside him. Scared the hell out of him and, paradoxically, made him yearn to hear it again.

* * * * *

*Discover how this rugged rancher's wanderlust
is tamed in time for a merry Christmas, in
A STONE CREEK CHRISTMAS.
In stores December 2008.*

Silhouette®

SPECIAL EDITION™

**FROM *NEW YORK TIMES*
BESTSELLING AUTHOR**

LINDA LAEL MILLER

A STONE CREEK CHRISTMAS

Veterinarian Olivia O'Ballivan finds the animals
in Stone Creek playing Cupid between her and
Tanner Quinn. Even Tanner's daughter, Sophie,
is eager to play matchmaker. With everyone
conspiring against them and the holiday season
fast approaching, Tanner and Olivia may just get
everything they want for Christmas after all!

*Available December 2008
wherever books are sold.*

SPECIAL EDITION™

Kate's Boys

MISTLETOE AND MIRACLES

by *USA TODAY* bestselling author

MARIE FERRARELLA

Child psychologist Trent Marlowe couldn't believe his eyes when Laurel Greer, the woman he'd loved and lost, came to him for help. Now a widow, with a troubled boy who wouldn't speak, Laurel needed a miracle from Trent...and a brief detour under the mistletoe wouldn't hurt, either.

Available in December wherever books are sold.

REQUEST YOUR FREE BOOKS!

2 FREE NOVELS PLUS 2 FREE GIFTS!

Silhouette® Romantic

SUSPENSE

Sparked by Danger, Fueled by Passion!

YES! Please send me 2 FREE Silhouette® Romantic Suspense novels and my 2 FREE gifts (gifts are worth about $10). After receiving them, if I don't wish to receive any more books, I can return the shipping statement marked "cancel." If I don't cancel, I will receive 4 brand-new novels every month and be billed just $4.24 per book in the U.S. or $4.99 per book in Canada, plus 25¢ shipping and handling per book plus applicable taxes, if any*. That's a savings of at least 15% off the cover price! I understand that accepting the 2 free books and gifts places me under no obligation to buy anything. I can always return a shipment and cancel at any time. Even if I never buy another book from Silhouette, the two free books and gifts are mine to keep forever.

240 SDN EEX6 340 SDN EEYJ

Name _____ (PLEASE PRINT)

Address _____ Apt. #

City _____ State/Prov. _____ Zip/Postal Code

Signature (if under 18, a parent or guardian must sign)

Mail to the **Silhouette Reader Service:**

IN U.S.A.: P.O. Box 1867, Buffalo, NY 14240-1867
IN CANADA: P.O. Box 609, Fort Erie, Ontario L2A 5X3

Not valid to current subscribers of Silhouette Romantic Suspense books.

Want to try two free books from another line?
Call 1-800-873-8635 or visit www.morefreebooks.com.

* Terms and prices subject to change without notice. N.Y. residents add applicable sales tax. Canadian residents will be charged applicable provincial taxes and GST. Offer not valid in Quebec. This offer is limited to one order per household. All orders subject to approval. Credit or debit balances in a customer's account(s) may be offset by any other outstanding balance owed by or to the customer. Please allow 4 to 6 weeks for delivery. Offer available while quantities last.

Your Privacy: Silhouette is committed to protecting your privacy. Our Privacy Policy is available online at www.eHarlequin.com or upon request from the Reader Service. From time to time we make our lists of customers available to reputable third parties who may have a product or service of interest to you. If you would prefer we not share your name and address, please check here. ☐

SRS08R

nocturne™

New York Times bestselling author

MERLINE LOVELACE

LORI DEVOTI

HOLIDAY WITH A VAMPIRE II

CELEBRATE THE HOLIDAYS WITH TWO BREATHTAKING STORIES FROM *NEW YORK TIMES* BESTSELLING AUTHOR MERLINE LOVELACE AND LORI DEVOTI.

Two vampires, each wary of human relationships, are put to the test when holiday encounters blur the boundaries of passion and hunger.

Available December wherever books are sold.

COMING NEXT MONTH

#1539 BACKSTREET HERO—Justine Davis
Redstone, Incorporated
When Redstone executive Lilith Mercer is nearly injured in two suspicious accidents, her boss calls in security expert Tony Alvera. But the street-tough, too-attractive *younger* agent is the last man Lilith wants protecting her as she faces her tarnished past. They get closer to the truth, and find that danger—and love—are hiding in plain sight.

#1540 SOLDIER'S SECRET CHILD—Caridad Piñeiro
The Coltons: Family First
They'd shared one night of passion eighteen years ago, but Macy Ward had never told anyone that Fisher Yates was the father of her son, T.J. Now Fisher is back in town, and when T.J. disappears, Macy turns to him for help. Will their search for their son reveal the passion they've been denying all these years?

#1541 MERRICK'S ELEVENTH HOUR—Wendy Rosnau
Spy Games
Adolf Merrick—code name Icis—has discovered a mole in the NSA Onyxx Agency, which has allowed his nemesis to stay one step ahead. In a plot to capture his enemy, Merrick kidnaps the man's wife—who mysteriously has his own dead wife's face! With the clock ticking and the stakes high, Merrick is in a race against time for the truth.

#1542 PROTECTED IN HIS ARMS—Suzanne McMinn
Haven
Amateur psychic Marysia O'Hurley figures her powers are the real deal when U.S. Marshal Gideon Brand enlists her help. The reluctant allies embark on a roller-coaster ride to rescue a little girl, with killers one step behind them. Even as they dodge bullets, will they find passion in each other's arms?

SRSCNMBPA1108